PROFESSOR ANDERSEN'S NIGHT

Dag Solstad

Professor Andersen's Night

TRANSLATED

FROM THE NORWEGIAN

BY

Agnes Scott Langeland

Harvill *Secker*

LONDON

Published by Harvill Secker 2011

2 4 6 8 10 9 7 5 3 1

Copyright © Dag Solstad 1996
English translation copyright © Forlaget Oktober 2011

Dag Solstad has asserted his right under the Copyright,
Designs and Patents Act 1988 to be identified as the author of this work

First published with the title *Professor Andersens natt* in 1996
by Forlaget Oktober, Oslo

First published in Great Britain in 2011 by
HARVILL SECKER
Random House
20 Vauxhall Bridge Road
London SW1V 2SA

www.randomhouse.co.uk

Addresses for companies within The Random House Group Limited
can be found at: www.randomhouse.co.uk/offices.htm

The Random House Group Limited Reg. No. 954009

A CIP catalogue record for this book is available from the British Library

ISBN 9781843432128

This translation has been published with the financial assistance of NORLA

The Random House Group Limited supports The Forest Stewardship Council (FSC®),
the leading international forest certification organisation. Our books carrying
the FSC label are printed on FSC® certified paper. FSC is the only forest
certification scheme endorsed by the leading environmental organisations,
including Greenpeace. Our paper procurement policy can be found at
www.randomhouse.co.uk/environment

Typeset in Bell MT by Palimpsest Book Production Limited,
Falkirk, Stirlingshire
Printed and bound in Great Britain by
Clays Ltd, St Ives plc

Professor Andersen's Night

I T WAS CHRISTMAS EVE and Professor Andersen had a Christmas tree in the living room. He stared at it. 'Well, I must say,' he thought. 'Yes indeed, I must say.' Then he turned and ambled round the living room, while he listened to the Christmas carols on TV. 'Yes, I must say,' he repeated. 'Hmm, yes, what shall I say?' he added, pondering. He looked at the tastefully laid table in the dining room. Laid for one. 'Weird how ingrained it is,' he thought, 'and so utterly devoid of irony, too,' he added, shaking his head. He was looking forward to dinner. Under the Christmas tree lay two presents, one from each of his grown-up nephews. 'If I say I hope I manage to get the crackling crisp, might there be a hint of irony in that? No,' he thought, 'if the crackling isn't perfect, I'll be furious, I shall swear out loud, even if it is Christmas Eve.' Just as he had sworn out loud when he had struggled to set up the tree on its base, and afterwards to make it stand straight and not lop-sided, like a tree should indoors. Just as he had done when he fastened the electric lights on to the branches of the tree, and discovered that this year, as usual, he had gone in circles, all the business with the wires, getting them entangled, so that he'd had to stop and unwind them, take off the lights one at a time and start all over again, almost right from the beginning. 'Damn,' he had said then. 'Damn.' Loudly, and clearly, but that was yesterday. 'Funny how Christmas Eve is so ingrained in us,' he thought. The solemnity. Holy Night. Which will come to pass at twelve o'clock tonight. Not before, as many people in Norway think; this is the evening before Holy Night. Or Silent Night. He went out into the kitchen. Opened the oven door. Took out the pork ribs. Inhaled the delectable aroma, and regarded the crisp crackling with satisfaction. Got everything ready, and carried it in for serving before he went into the bedroom and quickly changed his clothes. Came out again dressed in his good grey suit, white shirt, tie, well-polished black shoes. He sat down at the table to partake of his Christmas dinner.

Professor Andersen savoured his traditional Christmas meal. He ate pork ribs with surkål, vegetables, potatoes, prunes and whipped cranberries, as was the custom in the region of Norway he came from, and at the same time that most people throughout the country partook of Christmas dinner, some time between 5 and 7 p.m. He drank beer and aquavit, as one often does with this rich dish, which one seldom eats except at Christmas time. He ate slowly and ceremoniously, and drank thoughtfully. When he was finished, he carried the plate and the serving dishes out into the kitchen and carried in the dessert, which was creamed rice, another tradition in his family, although not particularly tasty, he thought. But he ate that, too, with ceremony. Afterwards he cleared the table and went into the living room, where he set out the coffee things on the little table in front of the fireplace. He lit the fire and sat down. Coffee and cognac. 'I'll skip the Christmas cakes,' he thought. 'Spare me the Christmas cakes. I'll just have to drink more coffee and cognac,' he chuckled contentedly. He stared at the lit-up Christmas tree, which was standing quite near the fireplace. Simply but tastefully decorated with tinsel and Norwegian flags in symmetrical rows around the tree. 'Most people decorate the tree far too much,' Professor Andersen said to himself. 'Well, that is usually when there are young children in the family,' he added in a conciliatory tone. He opened the presents from his nephews. One had given him a novel by Ingvar Ambjørnsen. The other had given him a novel by Karsten Alnæs. 'Well, well, so Christmas came round this year, too,' he thought, with a little sigh.

Professor Andersen felt at peace, tonight. He had this feeling of inner peace which was not of a religious but of a social kind. He liked to indulge in these Christmas rituals, which in fact meant nothing to him. He did not have to do it. He celebrated Christmas on his own, after all, and he was not tied to these customs with deep and sincere emotions; he could easily have managed without the Christmas tree, for instance, no one would have reacted to him not having a Christmas tree; on the contrary, the people he could count on visiting him during Christmas would be more likely to express surprise at him having a Christmas tree, and such a big Christmas tree, bigger than he was himself, in fact, and he might as well begin right now to dismiss the witticisms which would rain down on his poor head because of this, he thought and had to laugh. No, Professor Andersen had a Christmas tree, a Christmas tree somewhat bigger than he was; it had to be that big, he thought. He celebrated Christmas. Mainly because he felt very uneasy at the thought that he might have done the opposite. Not given a damn about anything connected to Christmas Eve, let Christmas be Christmas and dropped Christmas preparations and Christmas celebrations, and behaved as though it were any old day, and thereby gained an additional and sorely needed working day. Sat in his ordinary jeans and worked on a lecture, or seen to his correspondence, with which he was far behind, particularly the official part. Eaten meatballs with boiled cabbage in the kitchen, or one of the pasta dishes he was so good at making. Carried on with his own affairs and let others celebrate Christmas in their own way, in the thousands of homes where lights were lit. The idea that he could have done that, without arousing any particular reaction, upset him. In a way, he would have felt emotionally stunted if he were to do that. 'Yes, I would actually have felt emotionally stunted,' he thought defiantly, if somewhat surprised because that was, in fact, how it was. He could not reject Christmas; he had to observe the traditional customs. It was the right thing for him to do, anything else was quite out of the question, even though the customs he observed and the celebration he thereby took part in, in his own way and without any feeling of obligation to his family or others, beyond the feeling of duty he felt to himself, and that actually came from within, pointed to a meaning of some kind which for him was meaningless. Utterly alone, indeed without anyone even knowing about it, or caring about it, he took part in the celebration of the major Christian ceremony in memory of the Saviour's birth, and he felt a sense of inner peace from doing so, and for once he felt reconciled with his state of being, something he rarely had an opportunity to do, despite his high social rank and his position as professor of literature at the country's oldest university.

He sat in front of the fire and gazed into the flames. He threw the colourful Christmas paper from the two presents in the fire, and watched the flames flare up. He didn't throw the two gift tags into the fire, he kept them, mainly because he could not bring himself to throw away any personal greetings; after all, handwritten names on a gift tag must be called personal when all was said and done, he thought. He drank coffee and cognac. Gazed into the fire, lost in his own thoughts. Time passed. Now and then he went over to the window and stared out. At the empty street with the locked cars along the edge of the pavement in rows, and at the lights from the apartments opposite. Some of them were in darkness, apart from the faint lights on Christmas trees further within, which meant that the people who lived there had gone away, to their families, in order to celebrate Christmas Eve there. But other places were lit up. There, people were at home, celebrating Christmas. He noticed four apartments in particular where he could see that many people were gathered. For a second it annoyed him that he hadn't thought of going over to the window to stare at the apartments on the other side of the street while he was in the middle of his Christmas meal, as perhaps then he might have seen the four families sitting at the table at the same time, all of them within his field of vision, each in the light within their own apartments, right across from each other, and beside each other, distinctly separate, and without really knowing about each other, although they were gathered round the same thing, after all, and for the same ceremonial occasion. Oh, how he would have enjoyed that, the very sight of it, which would have struck him as familiar, a naive, confessional, civilised beauty, but now it was too late. Nevertheless, the scenes he was now able to observe in the four lit-up apartments were such that they filled him with a peculiar feeling of rapport. He could dimly see figures in all the apartments. Figures who were sitting in drowsy calm behind candles burning in seven-armed candlesticks in the window, or under glittering candelebras, or beside the dim lights on Christmas trees. He imagined the warm glow from their faces and bodies in there in the heated rooms, and an exhausting torpor, which transmitted itself to Professor Andersen as a familiar, drowsy calm. He felt a rapport with them. On this evening, as the hours moved towards twelve o'clock and the Holy Night was

[6]

about to begin, in which he wanted to take part, at least for a few short hours, even if they didn't give *that* a thought and he personally was also far removed from it, nevertheless there was now a rapport between Professor Andersen and those he was watching from his window, who were sitting in a drowsy torpor in their apartments, because they were all participants in this deep-rooted cultural ceremony, if not in the full sense felt by only a few here in the capital, then at least in time.

It must have been about eleven in the evening, an hour before what is called the Holy Night or Silent Night came to pass, a night celebrated on the same day in our country and in the other Nordic countries, though with the main emphasis on the previous evening, so-called Christmas Eve, celebrated for the same purpose, to commemorate the Holy Night when Jesus of Nazareth, the Saviour, was born in a stable in the town of Bethlehem in Judaea in the year which has been termed the year nought, that Professor Andersen stood like this staring across at the lighted apartments on the other side of the street, filled with this peculiar feeling of familiarity because they were all carried back to 2,000-year-old images tonight, whether they heeded it or not. In his mind's eye the desert sky was stretched over Judaea in the December of the year which starts our reckoning of time. The thousands of stars, which twinkled and twinkled in the deep blue sky. The shepherds in the fields outside Bethlehem. An angel standing in front of them and declaring tidings of great joy. Professor Andersen saw the angel in his mind's eye, in front of the shepherds and the sheep, lit up, and derived pleasure from visualising the angels, lit up in the dark night. He imagined he heard the angels praising God, and this, too, filled him with a strange sacred feeling. A crib in a stable. Mary and Joseph, dressed in smocks, bowing over it, and the shepherds kneeling, and the sheep looking at them. The large, yellow star of Bethlehem in the desert sky. The three wise men riding on camels through the desert, following the large star, coming to a halt outside the stable in Bethlehem. Kings of the Orient bowing in front of the crib. Gold, incense and myrrh. Oh, these images which he could allow himself to be captivated by with childlike delight, as images without deeper religious meaning. Godless devotion to these relics in an age where little or nothing seems to have the slightest opportunity to survive, going astray in the fog of history in a matter of seconds and ending up lost forever, thought Professor Andersen, with a little sigh. 'Here I stand, half-drunk and sentimental, and I am gripped by the Christmas scripture,' thought Professor Andersen. 'A 55-year-old professor who has opened his mind to his inner nature, and is thus enabled to imbibe ancient tales of religious origin, and a feeling of peace arises in his mind, is that how it is, perchance?' he wondered. 'Yes, it must be so,' he added. 'And let it be so,' he added further, thoughtfully. 'I am a non-believer, but belong to a Christian culture, and without a touch of irony I can let the Christmas spirit fill my mind. Soon it will be the Holy Night. But fortunately I have my limitations,' he thought next. 'I cannot utter the words "the Holy Child" without it automatically becoming "the Choly Hild", and I start to laugh,' he thought, and felt laughter bubbling up inside him. 'Nor can I utter "Jesus",' he added hurriedly in order to become serious again, 'without immediately having to add "of Nazareth"; "Jesus of Nazareth" I can cope with, but not just "Jesus". "The Saviour" I can say. "Christ" as well. If anyone asked me if I believe in Jesus, then I would cringe, but if anyone were to ask if I believe in Christ, then I wouldn't have any trouble answering politely and truthfully that no, I do not,' thought Professor Andersen, as he stared across at the lighted windows on the other side of the street. Saw the people sitting in their living rooms, with their lit-up Christmas trees, celebrating this 2,000-year-old event. 'Gripped by a ritual which for many of them means nothing, but which they cannot neglect to observe, in their finest attire, like me,' he thought. 'With a childlike nature. Yes, with a childlike nature,' he repeated, 'here in the far north, in the bleak midwinter, cold, in a modern capital city in a technologically advanced, wealthy country towards the end of the twentieth century,' he thought. 'Yes, a man ought to experience images of the Holy Night with his childlike sensibilities intact,' he thought, 'at least with a nod and a smile towards these aspects, or possibilities, in his innermost thoughts, encouraging their presence, rather than putting them in their place, as one often does, and often rightly so, too,' he added prosaically, while standing in front of the window in his apartment, waiting for the Holy Night to come to pass, a night he would spend an hour of, or perhaps two, sunk in reflection before he went to bed, or so he had decided, as he stood there in front of the window in his finest attire and stared at the lighted windows on the other side of the street.

But lo and behold a woman appeared at one of the windows. It did not belong to one of the four apartments he had under special surveillance that evening, but to one of the smaller apartments in the same building, which had been lit up the whole time, he had noticed, but without arousing his curiosity to any extent, maybe because the residents were sitting so far inside the apartment that it was impossible to get an impression of them. But now a woman was standing there. She was staring out of the window. She was beautiful, it occurred to Professor Andersen, standing there in the window with her long, fair hair, staring gravely straight in front of her. She need not be beautiful in reality, but from the way she appeared in the window, she seemed to be beautiful, with a slim, girlish figure and her long, fair hair. 'Young,' thought Professor Andersen, 'maybe an office worker, or someone who studies, either full-time or on the side.' He did not manage to observe her for long, however, for she turned round suddenly, because another figure appeared in the room behind her. It was a man; he, too, seemed to be young, although Professor Andersen was unable off-hand to say why he assumed the new figure to be a young man. 'But one is reasonably certain about that kind of thing, it strikes one immediately; it may

[10]

be something about the sprightliness with which he appeared on the scene, for instance,' he thought, before he reared back in horror as the man whom he had declared with such immediate certainty to be young put his hands around the woman's neck and squeezed. She flailed her arms about, Professor Andersen noticed, her body jerked, he observed, before she all at once became completely still beneath the man's hands and went limp. The young man straightened up, and Professor Andersen hurriedly hid behind his own curtains, for he saw that the young man was heading over to the window. When Professor Andersen peeked carefully from behind his curtain, he saw that the curtains in the other apartment had been drawn.

'I must call the police,' he thought. He went over to the telephone, but did not lift the receiver. 'It was murder. I must call the police,' he thought, but still did not lift the receiver. Instead he went back to the window. The curtains were still drawn in the window in the apartment on the other side of the street. Nothing indicated that anything unusual had happened there. Late Christmas Eve, the curtains drawn, quite common. 'But I saw it with my own eyes,' he groaned. 'I have witnessed a murder, I must let someone know.' He stared across at the window with the drawn curtains. He stared and stared. Thick curtains that did not let a glimpse of light in or out. 'What on earth has happened?' he thought. 'It is horrible really, and right in front of my eyes, too. I saw it with my own eyes, didn't I? Yes, I can describe it in detail. I must call the police.' He went over to the telephone, but didn't lift the receiver. 'What shall I say,' he thought, 'that I have seen a murder? Yes, that's what I have to say. And then they will laugh at me, and tell me to go and lie down, and to call back when I have sobered up, because it is a well-known fact,' he added, 'that when you have drunk a bit and try to sound sober, you may easily be considered fairly heavily intoxicated, because you get so anxious about sounding slurred that slurring positively takes hold of you. And so beside myself as I am now, it won't work.'

Instead, he stationed himself at the window, behind the curtain, with all the lights in his living room switched off, and kept watch on the window where he had seen a murder being committed. He stood thus for several hours, in the dark in his own living room, and stared. At the rectangular surface over there. Which shut out what he had seen. 'It is odd that I don't call the police,' he thought. 'It is still not too late. Even if they won't believe me, claim that I am drunk or whatever they may say, at any rate I would have reported it, and then it's up to them what they decide to do. It's as simple as that.' But he didn't go and call them. He stood at the window and stared. Stared across at the rectangular surface over there. Was he in there still? Probably, because he hadn't seen any man come out of the front entrance on his own. But he could have fled while Professor Andersen was over at the telephone. But then why would he have drawn the curtains? 'No, he has to be in there still,' thought Professor Andersen. 'Behind those thick curtains is a young man in the company of a dead woman, whom he has just murdered. And I know it,' he thought, 'but I'm not doing anything about it. I ought to have phoned, for my own sake, if for no other reason. It's curious. I know I should have done it, but I can't. That is how it is, I simply cannot do it.'

He continued to stare at the closed window, but also kept watch on the front entrance, in case the murderer should come out. But nothing happened. It was late at night, and Professor Andersen noticed that he was sleepy. What was he standing there for? To *see* if the curtains were suddenly drawn back again? Or if the murderer came out of the front entrance, so he could take a look at him? Why should he do that? What was the purpose of that? Did he have to see the man he was incapable of reporting to the police, so that he could be arrested for the murder he had just committed? Why on earth would he have to do that? Professor Andersen had to admit that he cherished an obsessive desire to *see* the murderer. Otherwise why would he be standing here at the window keeping a closer and closer eye on the front entrance? Because there was one thing of which he was certain: that he had fastened his gaze on that closed window for so long in the hope of seeing the curtains being drawn back, due surely to a crazy notion that everything would be as before, that the young woman would appear in the window, young and beautiful as before, for some reason or other, which he wouldn't need to speculate about. But when his eyes slipped towards the front entrance, it was to catch the murderer bounding away, not to see the impossible dream of the young couple coming out of it, whistling, on the night before Christmas Day; oh no, he didn't have the slightest belief in that at all, not even as an impossible hope; as his eyes now swept over the front entrance, it was to see the murderer bounding away, the murderer's face, an obsessive wish for that to happen. Nevertheless, Professor Andersen found this wish so distasteful that he decided not to stand there embroiled in the situation until he fulfilled this singular urge to see the murderer's face. So he went to bed.

He managed to sleep. Uneasily, to be sure, but he slept. He tossed and turned in bed, more or less in an uneasy doze, but he slept. Towards morning he woke up as he needed to get up and pee. He tumbled out, and went to the toilet. When he was finished, he tumbled back into bed, but only after making a detour through the living room, where he went over to the window and stared across at the apartment on the other side of the street. The curtain was still drawn. He went back to bed, and when he woke up, it was late in the day.

He went to the bathroom and showered. Put on the same suit as the day before, white shirt and a tie, black shoes, since it was Christmas Day, and went out into the kitchen to make breakfast. While he was laying the table in the dining room he walked over to the window and stared out. It had begun to snow. Large snowflakes were floating down from the sky and had covered the street and the pavement.

It seemed so peaceful that Professor Andersen felt a pang in his heart as he let his gaze rest on the window of the apartment straight across the street. The curtain was still drawn. He ate his Christmas breakfast, and decided afterwards to go for a walk in the snowy weather.

Professor Andersen had a roomy apartment in Skillebekk, a residential area down by the sea at Frognerkilen, but cut off from the sea first by the (now disused) railway line and then by the motorway, which is the main traffic route into West Oslo. There was a chill in the air, which hit him in the face as he came out of the entrance and turned round the corner into Drammensveien, while at the same time he noticed that the snow was falling thick and fast and was settling in his hair (he was bare-headed). The snow was already quite deep and it hadn't been cleared, except in Drammensveien itself, and a cheerful, resigned mood prevailed in the side streets, whilst car owners had great difficulties driving off in their cars, and since it was Christmas Day, and no real duties awaited anyone, this led to noisy agreement about the chaotic wintry conditions which the night's, or the early morning hours', snowfall had caused, and it all seemed terribly social to Professor Andersen as he stomped through the snow among all the cheerful people, who were drawing attention to their futile but demanding tasks. He walked up Niels Juels gate, to Bygdøy Allee, and from there further on towards Briskeby. He was only out for a walk, as were a great many others that Christmas morning. But even before he reached

Briskeby he decided to turn back. He couldn't bear to walk, he felt so heavy at heart. He was extremely restless. 'Oh,' he thought, 'I wish I had phoned after all, then this episode would have been over and done with. Then it would just have been an exciting episode, which would have been over as far as I was concerned. But now I'm so restless,' he thought, and decided to turn back.

For an instant, however, he wondered if he shouldn't carry on all the same, up towards Briskeby and from there along Briskebyveien in order to go up Industrigata to Majorstua and to the police station in Jacob Aalls gate. 'After all, I can report it now,' he thought. 'Then it is over and done with. Certainly I might run into some unpleasantness, because I haven't told them before, but everybody is bound to understand, if they just try to understand, that it can happen to the best of people.' For an instant he was so strongly tempted by the idea of carrying on up towards Briskeby, along Briskebyveien, right up to Majorstua police station, that he felt positively relieved by the very possibility of it. But no sooner had he felt this sense of relief coursing through his body than he realised that these were in any case just idle thoughts, which could cheer him up true enough, momentarily, but which he was never going to act on, and he decided once and for all to stop toying with such hypothetical ideas, which only led him deeper and deeper into the mire, or so he put it to himself, whilst he turned and walked back down Niels Juels gate towards Skillebekk again. He headed back home, anxious to see if anything had happened. He managed to stop himself looking over at the window in the other apartment building, while he himself was down on the street, in front of the building where he lived, with the other building on the other side of the street, and waited until he had unlocked the door at the front entrance and had gone up the stairs to his own apartment and let himself in there and gone over to the window. No. It was the same.

'Pull yourself together,' he told himself urgently. 'You have been gone for half an hour on Christmas morning, to be exact from 12.45 p.m. to 1.15 p.m.; how do you imagine that anything could have happened at the window in such a short space of time? Hope, well, yes, but it's a faint hope. Something will happen over there sometime, but it needn't happen today. Calm down. Think about something else.' But he could think of nothing else.

'I have to talk to someone,' he thought. 'I must call someone.' He thought about his friends, which of them he should call, and while he was thinking about it, he remembered that tomorrow, on Boxing Day, he was of course supposed to go to Nina and Bernt Halvorsen's place for dinner. 'I can wait till then,' he thought. 'I'll talk to Bernt about it. He is a doctor after all.' He was invited for seven o'clock, and if he arrived an hour earlier, then he and Bernt would have plenty of time to talk, while Nina was in the kitchen getting the food ready, he thought. Bernt most likely only has to see to the wine, uncork it and put it beside the heater to bring it to the right temperature, and while Bernt Halvorsen saw to that, he could explain. The thought of this calmed him. All he had to do was to stick it out for just over a day, and then he could explain. He'd manage that. He could bear it for that long. He went into the kitchen and had a look at the lutefisk he had in the fridge. Took it out and felt it. It was nice and firm, you can keep lutefisk in the fridge for a whole day, as long as you buy prime quality fish, he thought, and put the fish back in the fridge again. He wasn't going to dine until evening. In the meantime he was going to read a good book, whatever he meant by that, he thought. And along with the book he'd have a drink. With dinner: beer and aquavit. With the coffee: cognac.

And that was the way it turned out, you might say. Professor Andersen woke up the next morning with a bad hangover. It was still snowing. The roar of snowploughs could be heard everywhere, as well as the grating sound they made as they scraped the snow off the road surface on Drammensveien. The curtains in the window opposite were still drawn. The rectangular curtains which covered the whole window, in an extremely compact manner. Professor Andersen had repeatedly gone across and looked over at the other side of the street, yesterday Christmas Day, and last night, and he did so frequently this day, too. He was looking forward to the dinner party at Nina and Bernt Halvorsen's. As early as five in the afternoon he left his apartment, because he suddenly decided that he wanted to walk all the way to Sagene.

He walked up Niels Juels gate to Riddervolds Plass, after that up Camilla Colletts vei and Josefines gate to Homansbyen and Bislet. From Bislet: up Dalsbergstien to Ullevålsveien and St Hanshaugen, then steeply down Waldemar Thranes gate to Alexander Kiellands Plass. From there he walked along Maridalsveien up to Vøien Bridge, and up there, in a small house beside the River Aker whose grassy banks were now covered in snow, lived the Halvorsens, the married couple, both doctors, who had invited him to dinner. He walked along calmly at first, slowly, in fact, through the driving snow and the Yuletide darkness towards Riddervolds Plass and Bislet, because he had plenty of time and did not want to arrive too early; after all, he intended to arrive at six o'clock for a dinner he was invited to at seven. But even before he was at Bislet he noticed that his pace had quickened, because he had a burning desire to carry out his plan, and so, when he was at St Hanshaugen and about to start on the descent to Alexander Kiellands Plass, he felt good and warm and longed to reach his destination, so that he might give vent to the thoughts burning inside him. Because he knew why he had put himself in this situation. He couldn't have acted otherwise. He had witnessed a murder, and hadn't reported it. No, indeed, he had not. He didn't have the slightest inclination to do so, and he knew why. The murder had happened. That was the issue, something irreversible had happened, something he had witnessed. He couldn't warn them about something irreversible. If he had witnessed a burglary, had he, for instance, seen there were

[19]

thieves in that same apartment, who were carrying out a television and a stereo, then he wouldn't have hesitated to call the police. Because then it would have been urgent. Likewise if there had been a fire. If he had seen smoke seeping out of the window, or smelt it, he would, of course, have called the fire brigade without a moment's hesitation. And, well, if he had witnessed a vicious assault down on the street, and it had looked as though one of them was killing the other, then he would have run over to the phone and called the police. And while he waited for the police, he would have considered intervening himself in order to stop the abuse, if he hadn't been too cowardly, that is. Well, let's say that he had been too cowardly, and one person had battered the other to death before the police arrived, while he stood and watched it, then he would it is true have had dreadful pangs of conscience to contend with, but he could have lived with that, yes, he damn well could live with that, he thought defiantly, and, coward or not, he would certainly have called the police. There was no doubt about that, because that phone call could have prevented something irreversible happening. But he had been a witness to something irreversible, and there was nothing he could do. He couldn't make things better by calling to notify them that it had happened. The murder, which he'd witnessed, was an accomplished fact. 'I can't tell them about this. The only outcome would be the murderer's arrest.' And the murderer might well be caught, but not on account of him, Professor Andersen, intervening and notifying them that the man had committed a murder. The idea was distasteful to him.

'Do you understand what I'm saying?' he thought, directed to the people whose house he was now hastening towards. 'The young woman will never stand in the window again. Maybe I have been hoping for two days that she will stand in the window again, but she isn't going to. She is dead. She is murdered. The curtains are drawn. And when they get drawn back, it will be the murderer who is standing in the window, peering out. It's impossible for me to play a part in his capture. I can't commit such an offence against a man who has murdered,' he thought, horrified at what he was actually thinking, but at the same time longing to talk about it to a friend, so he hurried up Maridalsveien. Yes, he almost ran through the snowy weather and the winter darkness and the city's lights, for an opportunity to share his opinion on the irreversible thing that had happened.

He was out of breath when he rang the doorbell at the Halvorsens'. Bernt opened it. 'Heavens, are you here already?' he exclaimed. 'Yes, wasn't it at seven o'clock then?' answered Professor Andersen innocently. 'Yes, but it's a quarter to six now,' said Bernt, and he laughed. 'Oh, damn, I must have got the time wrong,' muttered Professor Andersen. Bernt opened the door wide, and Professor Andersen shuffled in, crestfallen. This wasn't how he had imagined it. He had thought that when Bernt Halvorsen looked surprised and said that he had come far too early, that he would, of course, have answered: 'Yes, I know that, but I have something important to talk to you about.' Why had he not said that?

Maybe because it struck him as being a little impetuous. He had, after all, enough time before the other guests arrived to talk to Bernt about this. He would try to bring the conversation round to it in a natural way. But that proved to be impossible. He couldn't bring himself to talk about it, even though he and Bernt had ended up sitting in the living room with a drink each (as he had imagined in advance), while Nina was out in the kitchen making food, now and then asking her husband to come and help with something or other. Each time Bernt went into the kitchen, Professor Andersen had an abundance of time to consider how he might ease the conversation round to the subject he was dying to tell a friend in confidence, either by summoning up his courage and coming straight to the point, or by finding a lead which would allow Professor Andersen to drop an opportune remark lightly and easily, even though it was dreadful. But when Bernt Halvorsen returned to the living room, that remark did not present itself. The time was getting on for 7 p.m., and the other guests would soon be arriving. Professor Andersen expected the doorbell to ring. The doorbell might just as well ring. Because he understood. He knew now; he wasn't able to confide in his good friend Bernt Halvorsen, not about this. About a lot of other things, but for some reason or other not about this.

The other guests arrived. They were all acquaintances of Professor Andersen. There was the actor Jan

Brynhildsen, who had become a marvellous interpreter of comic roles at the National Theatre, and his second wife, the somewhat faded air hostess Judith Berg, and there was the senior psychologist Per Ekeberg and his partner Trine Napstad, the top civil-service administrator in the Ministry of Culture. All the guests were in their fifties like their hosts Nina and Bernt Halvorsen, and had known each other for years. Professor Andersen was glad Nina and Bernt hadn't invited an additional female guest, who would have been his table companion, as he thought it much easier to relate to social occasions without having imposed on him the duty of entertaining a single woman, who, in advance, one had to assume, had looked forward to an eventful evening, and whose expectations he therefore would have had to do his utmost not to disappoint. He felt much freer as a single guest without a single woman accompanying him at the table, it also made him wittier, because then he could throw himself into the role of being an affable participant in the party as a whole, instead of having to be a tense, though gallant, cavalier.

They sat down at the dinner table. The seating arrangement had been fixed elegantly and with an experienced hand so that their being an odd number went unnoticed, but gave them an added sense of well being, since Nina, their hostess, had two companions at the table, Jan Brynhildsen, sitting on her left, and Per Ekeberg on her right, both of whom could then cheerfully compete to win her favour and attention, while Bernt, their host, had one female companion, Judith Berg, on his left, who for her part could enjoy this, while at the same time she had Per Ekeberg on her left. Trine Napstad could likewise enjoy having Professor Andersen as a table companion, but she also had Jan Brynhildsen, the comedy actor with leading roles at the National Theatre, on her right side, and he could converse with her if, or rather when, their hostess Nina was deep in conversation with Per Ekeberg sitting on her right, and in that way was able to relieve Professor Andersen, who then could take the opportunity to exchange a few words with his old friend Bernt Halvorsen, the host, whom he had sitting on his left, or just to stare vacantly into space, if the latter was deep in conversation with Judith Berg, his table companion. In this manner the conversation could flow easily from one to the other, with plenty of opportunity for all of them to get involved in one single topic, if most found it sufficiently interesting, because the responsibility of having a fixed female table companion hadn't been laid on anyone, apart from Bernt, but since he was the only one, a clear responsibility rested on him to ensure that the whole table was engaged in conversation, and preferably the same one at that, and thus it was evident yet again that on social occasions it is an advantage, and not a drawback, to have an odd number, thought Professor Andersen, and therefore it is so peculiar that those who take it upon themselves to invite people to a party worry time and again very much about inviting couples; remarkable, thought Professor Andersen, who could scarcely recall the last time he had been at a successful dinner party with an even number seated round the table.

They had rakfisk as a starter and the main course was grouse. Beer and a chaser of aquavit were served with the rakfisk; a Spanish red wine, a good Rioja, with the grouse. Before the starter was served, Nina their hostess complained of an irresolvable problem which they had encountered while drawing up the menu. Rakfisk as a starter, and grouse afterwards, they go together, not least if one considers that both the rakfisk and the grouse come from the same geographical area, Valdres. But as for the beverages, beer and a chaser of aquavit first, followed by red wine – Nina didn't think that was an ideal combination, but what else could they have done? Thought of a different starter before the grouse? No, she didn't want to do that, she said, when one has rakfisk in one's larder from Valdres, and grouse from the same area, both of them obtained in a personal way, considering that Bernt had shot the grouse, right there in Valdres, and the rakfisk was procured by one of their close acquaintances in Valdres, so it had to be done like this, 'And so you will just have to put up with drinking beer and a chaser with the rakfisk now, and going over to red wine later,' said Nina decidedly.

They ate rakfisk. They skolled with beer and aquavit. Professor Andersen was at a Christmas dinner party at his good friends' Nina and Bernt Halvorsen. Bernt he had known ever since his youth, and they had grown up together in a town somewhere near the Oslo Fjord. They had come to Oslo to study at the same time, Bernt medicine and he the arts and humanities, and they had remained close throughout their student days, despite belonging to different faculties. After a while Bernt found his Nina, who also studied medicine, and Professor Andersen had got to know her too. He had found a wife who also studied the arts and humanities, and from the end of their student days the two newly married couples had spent much time together. They had continued to see each other often, with intervals when one or other of the couples had been living outside Oslo – Nina and Bernt because they worked at a hospital out of town, he because he was abroad, either on a research grant or as a Norwegian visiting professor in Strasbourg, right up until he got divorced ten years ago, and then he had continued to see Nina and Bernt on his own. Both he and Bernt had been successful in life, he had secured a post at the university early on, had done a PhD and become a professor while still relatively young, at the same time as Bernt had made a career for himself in the hospital sector, where as a young man he had become a consultant, a position he held today at Ullevål Hospital.

The other guests were Nina and Bernt's friends, but for that reason they had also become close acquaintances of Professor Andersen. Per Ekeberg he remembered well, as a psychology student from the early Sixties, and also Trine Napstad he remembered from the dozy reading rooms at Blindern, where she, like him, had studied the arts and humanities. Small and animated, she had talked non-stop in a far-too-loud, piercing voice the moment she escaped the silence of the reading room. That had grated on his nerves somewhat, he remembered, even though he had thought she was attractive enough. When he had met her again, at Nina and Bernt's, as Per Ekeberg's new partner, and thus, in reality, his second wife, he on occasion found himself wondering about Per Ekeberg's first wife, since Per had settled down, found solace, with this woman on his journey through life, which also for him, Per Ekeberg, has an unavoidable conclusion, as we all know, and which, at least for brief periods of time, cannot fail to cause us concern. Per Ekeberg was a senior psychologist. It was a title he took with him when he moved from the public sector into private enterprise to be a director in the Norwegian branch of an international advertising agency. He appeared to be just as content in the private sector as he had been in the public one, and in addition he earned a lot more money, and it's possible he also set greater store by the creative side of his new profession, which, among other things, was such that he didn't need to call himself Director, but could continue to present himself as senior psychologist, which undoubtedly seemed more intriguing when the title was used in an advertising context.

If he were to choose, then he had greater respect for Jan Brynhildsen and Judith Berg than Per Ekeberg and Trine Napstad. Jan Brynhildsen had, as a newly divorced 45-year-old (after being married to a female colleague who at that time was far more successful than he was), fallen head over heels in love with an air hostess. A rather weary-looking beauty in her forties, who was a single mother with a teenage daughter from a short-lived affair with an Italian business magnate. Jan Brynhildsen was at the time a typical second-rate actor and his falling in love with a faded air hostess undeniably had a strong element of comedy to it, of the more malicious kind that Professor Andersen, for his part, couldn't claim to be entirely innocent of being partial to. But in this amorous project Professor Andersen had been Jan Brynhildsen's secret admirer. He had looked up to him, and inwardly urged him on, Jan Brynhildsen, the walk-on actor at the National Theatre, to follow the convictions of his heart. 'The person who is unable to be fascinated by his youthful dream of the Air Hostess has lost the ability to love,' he inwardly urged, 'even if she, Judith Berg, doesn't resemble the dream of the Air Hostess, but is a tired, middle-aged woman with a bad back and swollen feet and bitter wrinkles round her painted mouth, she nevertheless represents the Air Hostess, for whom we just have to fall, Jan Brynhildsen and I,' thought Professor Andersen, then as now. 'Jan Brynhildsen is ingenuous in his love, and for that I admire him, and he will surely be rewarded,' Professor Andersen had thought. And he had been rewarded. On stage. On the main stage at the National Theatre. That was where he now had his success. First in small roles, which all of a sudden were played with a comic talent that aroused interest among theatregoers. Very minor roles from the pens of great playwrights often have great comic potential which is seldom exploited, either because minor roles are played by minor actors or, if they are given to good actors, they can easily overshadow major roles and more important scenic events, and thus damage the dramatic unity of the piece. But Jan Brynhildsen succeeded, and that was because he didn't play the comic parts like a great actor, but like a minor one. He stood there in his minor role, completely devoid of dreams and ambitions. He didn't try to show the comic nature inherent in the character by stealing the scene. He stood there on the fringe, playing the minor role as a minor actor, but with luminous, raw, indeed hoarse, comedy, which many in the audience experienced as a magic moment of silence and laughter. Soon he was getting larger comic roles, and now he was one of the theatre's leading comic talents, who came to mind for a main part every time the theatre was to stage Molière, Holberg or a light comedy by Shakespeare. But although he gave a good performance in these classic comic roles – not least by continuing to preserve the minor actor in the garb of the leading role – it was the sweet (in the original meaning of the word) element of the character that was really touching, and one ought to be touched when seeing a comedy performed, but it was nevertheless Professor Andersen's opinion that it was in the minor parts that Jan Brynhildsen had carried out remarkable feats, and there were many people who were of the same opinion, even if this wasn't expressed publicly or privately by

Professor Andersen, because he didn't want to hurt Jan Brynhildsen, even though Jan Brynhildsen himself wouldn't have heard what he said.

They ate rakfisk. Drank beer with a chaser. Skolled and laughed, and chatted cheerfully. They all belonged to the same generation, and they were linked to each other by strong ties, even Professor Andersen, who, tonight in particular, struggled with a disturbing feeling that he had now parted from them for good. He still felt bowled over at being unable to confide in his friend Bernt, their host, when he had come to this dinner party an hour and a quarter early for the sole purpose of doing so. He now sensed that he was not just about to be, but already was tangled up in something which had consequences he couldn't imagine, and which were such that they threatened for one thing to leave him friendless, since it was now impossible for him to deny that the strong urge he had felt to confide in a friend, frankly, baring his soul, in reality couldn't be fulfilled when standing face to face with Bernt. This distracted Professor Andersen somewhat, and in this distracted frame of mind it would have been easy for him not to take part in this dinner group and to regard it from the position of an outsider, as if it were a remote event which didn't concern him, with gestures and rituals performed by strangers who didn't concern him, but that wasn't the outcome. Whether he wanted to or not, he belonged in the company of these successful intellectuals in their fifties in the capital of Norway towards the end of the twentieth century. They were linked to each other by such strong ties that, for instance, Professor Andersen, who wasn't a close friend of either Per Ekeberg or Trine Napstad, knew both of them from the university at Blindern in the Sixties, and that at a time when Per Ekeberg and Trine Napstad hadn't the foggiest notion of each other's existence, though she, Trine Napstad, easily remembered Per Ekeberg's first wife, who had been a childhood friend of Nina Halvorsen, at the time when her name was Nina Hellberg, which was still her name when Trine Napstad came to know her. Thus one could look back to the early Sixties, and the random, but strong and active, ties created at the university, where all of them had studied (apart from Judith Berg, who was at the time unattainable, an Air Hostess), and each in some way had become a radical student. None of them, apart from Jan Brynhildsen, had ever ended up on the far left, the revolutionary Marxist-Leninists, the Maoists, in the legendary – or notorious, if you prefer – Marxist-Leninist Workers Front known as AKP (M-L); they were, in fact, slightly too old for the likes of that, and too set in their ways when it came to the fore, but they had been anti-NATO and voted against the Common Market, relatively early in the Sixties, and early in the Seventies, and Per Ekebeg had demonstrated against apartheid at Madserud during a tennis tournament between Norway and South Africa, and had been carted off by the police, and Nina and Bernt had been anti-nuclear demonstrators and worn Ban the Bomb buttons on their duffle coats. The nuclear badge, as Andersen, still an undergraduate, had called it, alluding to the swimming badge so popular in their schooldays. 'I see you've earned your nuclear badge,' he would say, but neither Nina nor Bernt had laughed, for some things were too serious to make jokes about, and thus he had been left standing there with his silly joke, feeling silly himself as well when the others didn't laugh, for he was radical, too, in his way. However, as an undergraduate, Andersen's radicalism was mainly expressed through his interest in and his support of people who attacked either in speech or in writing the empirical school of thought, which was then the prevailing approach within philosophy and the social sciences, not to mention his preoccupation with all kinds of avant-garde trends in art and literature.

While Bernt Halvorsen was deeply preoccupied with the armaments race and the Cold War and was keen to take action, as an undergraduate Pål Andersen sat at home in his bedsit reading strange poems, which he had great difficulty interpreting. Was this his form of political radicalism, which linked him to the same life nerve that surged through Bernt Halvorsen with such unbending seriousness? Indeed, his preoccupation with avant-garde French and Polish films, modern literature and abstract paintings was an attempt, a desperate one at times, to enter the same period to which Bernt Halvorsen already belonged, and which he could defend from the inside with such accuracy. He was zealous in his efforts to understand avant-garde art, that form of art which has really taken hold of our own day and age.

He often felt that he had failed to understand it, indeed, more often than he would admit, it left him in a state of incomprehension, confusion, indifference, even after he had used all his astuteness to understand only a snippet of it. It could make him feel desperate. He felt a failure because he didn't understand the art of his own period, and it can't be denied that in such situations he often pretended to understand more than he actually understood, and even feigned an admiration for works of art which, in actual fact, left him unmoved. But on the other hand, what pleasure he could experience if, after a long struggle with, for instance, a modernist poem, he suddenly understood it! He had, for that matter, felt the greatest joy when he understood intuitively, directly. Why? Because then his own searching and restless and frequently maladjusted soul melded, as though it were the most natural thing in the world, with the greatest minds of his time. He had felt enlightened, and at the very highest level. It gave him a deep, tranquil satisfaction, as he had been moved by reality, and he hoped intensely that someone would pay a visit to his bedsit right then, so he could have read this poem aloud to them. That this reality had dissolved all conventional and normal reality, and depicted a quite different and often uncompromising reality, where ordinary things had ended up in unaccustomed and frightening positions, often accompanied by black humour, on this passage through a landscape of deformity and impossibility, of anxiety and pent-up screams, cynical and relentless, disparaging and dissolved, unnerved and alcoholised, fatally wounded by the belief in total happiness, none of that diminished Pål Andersen's pleasure at being able to understand the most outstanding achievements of his own day and age, but that the young man who took all this to his breast could, simultaneously, identify with serious and morally incensed political radicalism may well strike one as rather mysterious. But that is how it was. Pål Andersen's rare moments of happiness when he thought he understood the chaotic and iconoclastic form of an avant-garde work of art strengthened, rather than weakened, his confidence in his own impossible life, as a young man with the future ahead of him. He didn't seek comfort, but relentlessness. He didn't seek the structure he was brought up to see and understand, but the disintegration of that structure. He didn't turn to art in order to receive, but to see. He couldn't imagine using the word 'rewarding' about a work of art – for instance, that such and such a book has given me so much, taught me so much, etc. etc. – but thought solely that it enlightened him, made him see, cynically and without false expectations, so that he felt he was alive, something that young men often struggle to feel clearly, and which very easily makes them become maladjusted. Actually, it is not all that difficult to see that as a young man Andersen must have been a snob. If he were to become a part of his own day and age, with all his maladjustments, then it would have to be through reaching the highest level of enlightenment, through an understanding of this day and age's most outstanding achievements within the arts. But Professor Andersen would probably in any case have asked us to bear with him, especially when we now see his desperate attempts to relate to the avant-garde movement of his period, which for him was identical to modernity; being a young man of his own day and age, as he painstakingly tried to understand a poem by, for instance, Pound or Elouard, by Celan or Prévert, and then managed it, he succeeded, perhaps even intuitively; can't we visualise the leap in his own self-esteem when it takes place, and let us grant him that, and thereby the pride which rushes through this callow young man, who, in his deeply tranquil satisfaction, now has only one wish beyond the one which has already come his way, that someone would come and visit him, so that he might have someone to share this satisfaction with, therefore he wishes that someone would come, so that he can read this poem aloud for them here in his simple bedsit. Two youths, one of whom reads poetry to the other, two young students, one of whom reads aloud to the other from the works of their common youthful contemporaries with the most outstanding awareness of life as it is, and thereby also of life in the future. Pål Andersen wasn't young in the sense that he felt life-giving sap threatening to burst his veins. He didn't feel particularly strong, with unparalleled vigour, which was straining to get out, the way young people are often portrayed by older people, as a measure of youth, and which consequently has to be demonstrated through youthful conduct. He was a sallow youth, who smoked forty cigarettes a day, and drank five or six pints of beer in smoky, muggy bars three to four evenings a week, and who woke up with a hangover at least twice a week, so that it was a painful effort to drag himself up to the university at Blindern and his daily toil in reading rooms and in lecture theatres. He spent his life in stuffy surroundings, with flagging, aching limbs and endless brooding; nonetheless, it was beyond doubt that his young mind could respond, and that due to this responsiveness a promising future lay ahead of him. Now and then he was visited by his total opposite, the medical student Bernt Halvorsen, and then he read him poems, by Georg Johannesen for instance. Or by Stein Mehren, two Norwegian poets who were only a few years older than himself, and whom he admired enormously. Sitting on his unmade bed, with bedclothes that were never aired (but now and then actually washed), he read poems for Bernt.

Later, Georg Johannesen and Stein Mehren came to represent two opposite poles of Norwegian poetry, the former cultivated by high-brow left-wingers, the latter considered the greatest Norwegian poet since Wergeland by the conservatively minded; but in the early Sixties, when Andersen was reading them as an undergraduate and they were new, their poems belonged to the same frame of reference, at least for a young man who desperately leaned towards the avant-garde in order to feel he truly existed. When Pål Andersen read the following lines by Georg Johannesen aloud to Bernt Halvorsen: 'I am glad / I cannot see / my death in a mirror – When my picture falls down from the wall / I'll resemble the wallpaper / and when an heir counts my sheets / they will be white and clean / like the day I bought them – Everything has to be written anew / like before I wrote my signature,' and later the following lines by Stein Mehren: 'But the stranger who stands up on the hillside, listening / to the drone of a city by night. He can do nothing / He, too, is an observer. Through the night air / it looks as though the towns on the coast have been accidentally / washed ashore. And now lie there twisting con- / voluted like jellyfish of light – Far away . . . Far above hover the new gods / in the invisible spokes of the celestial wheel / From afar the towns can be seen as large / gently vibrating circles which interminably / spread their SOS,' then he was perfectly aware that these two poets differed greatly in their language and outlook, something he, in fact, also expressed by reading them in highly different ways to his friend Bernt Halvorsen: Georg Johannesen in a staccato, hoarse voice; Stein Mehren in a meandering, almost ecstatic voice (the way he had heard Stein Mehren himself read his own poems on the radio). But they had one thing in common, they were both *his* poets, and could invigorate his own life force, and he now read them eagerly for Bernt, purely as a matter of course, in order to hear his opinion.

And Bernt lent an ear. He listened, but if Pål Andersen waited eagerly to hear his friend's thoughts, hoping that his own enthusiasm might have instilled itself in Bernt Halvorsen's frame, he must have been disappointed. Because it never happened, and this was something young Andersen must have anticipated, and for that reason his intention couldn't have been to hear Bernt's enthusiastic interpretation when he read so eagerly; instead it must have been to get the feeling that Bernt listened, properly and politely, open to what so preoccupied his friend Pål, so that he might receive fresh acknowledgement of something he took so superbly for granted, since he, purely as a matter of course, invited his friend to a poetry reading from his ever-increasing repertoire of avant-garde writers, among whom were his Norwegian heroes Georg Johannesen and Stein Mehren, those young contemporaries, also to feel that he and Bernt were on the same side, and that being on the same side meant that Bernt listened with a genuinely open mind to Pål Andersen reading poetry, regardless of whether the poems were performed in a staccato, hoarse voice or in a meandering, ecstatic one. They were, as it happened, on the same side, and belonging to that side gave him the right to read avant-garde poetry to someone who was only mildly interested in it.

It was natural for him, Pål Andersen, to share Bernt Halvorsen's opposition to NATO and nuclear armament, even though he wasn't really so hugely preoccupied with it; it concerned him more as a topic of conversation than it did as a political action to which he himself had to ascribe, but he liked to listen while Bernt made his acute observations, occasioned by some topical political event, such as the Cuban crisis in 1962, and then make a couple of remarks, which showed that he agreed, or ask a few questions, which showed that he was attentive; that was perfectly natural for him, just as it was natural for Bernt to say, after he had listened to Pål Andersen reading 'Expectation' by Stein Mehren: That was really not bad at all; or when he read from 'Generation' by Georg Johannesen: Yes, that was rather good, as a token of approval. Although he never got round to buying any of these poetry collections himself, in order to read them himself, or aloud to Nina, and it was equally improbable that young Andersen would wear in his lapel the Ban the Bomb badge which Bernt had donated to him, and instead laid it on top of the chest of drawers in his bedsit, putting it openly and naturally on view, visible to everyone who came to visit. This naturalness was both a token of the fondness one had for things with which one was preoccupied and passionately interested in, and of the slightly polite distance, or regard, one showed towards the matters with which the other was preoccupied and passionately interested in, and was an expression of the fact that through them both flowed the same life force, which was theirs, and only theirs, the life force of their own day and age, the communal spirit of their generation. But only some of this generation; as a matter of fact most young people belonged among the stolid conservative types, with their rituals, which Bernt and Pål disliked, and even despised; they themselves were only a small minority but were distinctive enough to constitute a whole generation, about that they agreed whole-heartedly, both Pål Andersen and

Bernt Halvorsen. What they shared was directed at *them*, at the others, who were pro-NATO, who were for nuclear armament, and against avant-garde art. Perhaps not all of those who demonstrated, for instance, against apartheid and the tennis tournament between Norway and South Africa at Madserud were so fervently preoccupied with abstract art or incomprehensible free verse, perhaps many of them didn't appreciate it all that much, but they weren't shocked by it, they didn't get upset, they didn't shun avant-garde art, not even when it resulted in a Korean pianist smashing the piano as the finale of his concert in the University Assembly Hall; it didn't upset them, the way it upset *them*, the others, they would merely have commented on it by asking: Did he really do that?

In their own way all of the participants in this dinner party (all bar Judith Berg, who at this point in time still flew like a princess, not waited on, but waiting on, high up in the air above them somewhere, wonderfully beautiful) were within this alliance who shared radical political attitudes and a preoccupation with (or polite regard for) avant-garde art, in other words, members of the special minority who represented the New, modernity, the distinctive modernity of their time, and who cultivated being in opposition, against *them*, and the fine arts in a new, diluted form (in provincial Norway).

This was in the Sixties, more than thirty years ago. Now they were in a completely new phase of life. Life no longer lay ahead of them, they were no longer in the phase where you couldn't think 'I' without at the same time having the word 'future' in mind, but could allow themselves to look back and register that they had succeeded fairly well, as doctors, psychologists, leading actors, professors and cultural administrators. They were all in their fifties and all of them had grown-up children, apart from Professor Andersen, who was childless. But it was only their hosts Nina and Bernt Halvorsen who had children with each other. Senior pyschologist Per Ekeberg had children with his first wife, and they were now studying at the University of Oslo, psychology like their father, both the boy and the girl, while Trine Napstad's daughter was reading media studies in Volda. Judith Berg's daughter with the Italian business magnate had established a career as a TV presenter, and now had her own entertainment show on one of the TV channels. Nina and Bernt had three children: their son Morten, twenty-seven, who had left medical school to be a rock musician (as Bernt said, in reality he had become a pop musician); their son Thomas, twenty-five, who was nearing the end of his medical studies; and their daughter Clara Eugenie, fifteen, who was still at home, but who, of course, was out this particular evening. Whether Jan Brynhildsen had children, from his first marriage or in another way, was a little unclear.

If any of those present had taken photographs of the dinner group, what would you have seen? Immediately after they were developed, those who were there, the seven people around the table, the hosts and the five guests, would have recognised themselves and smiled a little at their own traits; and then have been even more amused, perhaps, by the other guests' traits; all seven of them would, in other words, have been concerned with both their own and the others' mannerisms, and in doing so given acknowledging smiles. But in thirty or thirty-five years' time the same picture, now in a photo album belonging to, let's say, Nina and Bernt's son Thomas, might perhaps, while he was showing it to his own children, who are in their twenties, call forth smiles of acknowledgement from Thomas, too, and his young sons (or daughters if you like), but now because this photo is so typical of the period. Typical of the Nineties, the time when Nina and Bernt Halvorsen were in their prime, and typical of this period in that set, that social grouping, which was theirs. They, that is Nina and Bernt's heirs, would look at the photo of these seven people around a dinner table, in old-fashioned clothes, in strange positions, and they would exclaim, even though the original photograph was supposed to have been taken spontaneously, so the people being photographed didn't know they were being photographed just then: So stiff they look, so arranged, and in spite of the fact that the very generation who were photographed here, and precisely this social grouping, with their shared development and background, were such that they individually and as a group were particularly pre-occupied with this very thing – trying to appear natural, relaxed, indeed spontaneous in every way, for such is the relentless nature of an image frozen in time; the rigid, the arranged is always apparent, and probably this rigid, unnatural, arranged look was actually the prevailing state of affairs at the time when the photo was taken, and of which they were such utter prisoners without noticing it themselves, but which now, an imagined thirty or thirty-five years on in time, streams out of the picture and brings about the feeling which calls forth the good-natured smiles we all adopt when we see photos from a time which isn't our own, and which you can call smiles of acknowledgement because one acknowledges what was typical of the Nineties in this chance photograph from a party on Boxing Day at their grandparents' house at Sagene, and taken before they, in other words Nina and Bernt's second-generation offspring, were even born. But while, let's say, Bernt Halvorsen, on taking a look at this photograph of himself, would have shaken his head, because he would at once have recognised some habits from his medical profession which he never managed to exclude from his private life, which therefore had to be called bad habits in such a setting and which he regarded as slightly comic, though obviously it was much too late to do anything about them now, at this stage in his life, such things as laying one hand over the other, originally to calm patients, but now one of his characteristic traits, even when he was hosting a party in his home on Boxing Day, he could only shake his head in partial resignation, before he went on to study the rest of the people in the photograph, his wife's little idiosyncrasies which came to light in the photo, and Per Ekeberg's intense way of leaning forward, or Professor Andersen's way of slightly tilting his head, which undeniably gave him an arrogant look, so typical of Pål, Bernt would have thought then, and smiled, because he knew that this arrogant, tilted head was a posture, created and built up to conceal the deep social insecurity that the 55-year-old had felt all his life, in the same way that his grandchildren, looking at the photograph in, for instance, the year 2029, would think how typical when they regarded their grandfather and Professor Andersen respectively, but they wouldn't think how typical of Grandfather, and how typical of Professor Andersen, but would exclaim, at the sight of them both: So typical of the Nineties to hold his hands like that, and his head like that! The spirit of the times operates like this, concealed from the person who is its prisoner, but apparent to someone who observes us in photographs from another period, liberated, from the outside.

There must undoubtedly have been something about this party in the home of a married couple who were both successful doctors in Oslo in the Nineties which would lead you to point to it and exclaim: Typical Nineties, even though both the hosts and the guests spontaneously expressed their individuality. What that might be would have been difficult (not to say impossible) for them to determine themselves, and, of course, so painful (herein lies the impossibility of it) that one would rather not be preoccupied with it, but Professor Andersen was thrown suddenly into a strange inner (and outer) existence which led, for one thing, to a strong feeling of unease about his own position within this group, in which he felt partially at home, not least because he knew its social codes, in other words what was regarded as good taste, the sense of humour, if you like, but in which he also felt partially trapped, so that he really would have liked to break out, in a tremendous act of will, in a tremendous leap, if that had been possible.

What was it that united them as a group that was easily recognisable as quite definitely belonging to that period? What, in other words, was their mark of distinction? Their individual development and individual lives had in many ways been similar to the development you would have found in any social grouping like the one to which they belonged. Success had made them adapt. Good food, good drink, spacious living accommodation, holiday houses and weekend homes, cars and boats set their mark on the privileged people who enjoy such benefits, radical or non-radical. But if this generation or, to be more precise, this small minority within their own age group, who were confident, and probably justly so, that they were right to claim their own hallmarks as hallmarks of their generation, for if they had any hallmarks to speak of, any small but important detail that made them stand out amongst other fifty-year-old professors, medical consultants, celebrated actors, heads of administration, senior psychologists who were radical youths in 1950 or 1970 or for that matter whatever one may predict will exist among fifty-year-olds in 2020, then it must have been their refusal to be pillars of society. They were strongly disinclined to regard themselves as pillars of society. Because they didn't feel they conformed: not to the authority, or rather duties, which they enacted, nor to the social group to which they belonged. They denied being what they were. They didn't feel that they conformed to their given status. They were consultants, heads of administration, senior psychologists, celebrated actors and professors of literature, but in their innermost thoughts they believed, every single one of them, that they had not adopted the attitude that was expected of them. They were still against *them*, the others, although they could scarcely be distinguished from them any longer, apart from in small ways; they liked to wear blue denim trousers, so-called jeans or Levi's, when they carried out their duties as heads of administration, professors, etc.; indeed, Professor Andersen himself rather liked to dress in jeans, and did so with glee, when he turned up at meetings at the National Theatre, where he was a board member. They continued to be against authority, deep inside they were in opposition, even though they were now, in fact, pillars of society who carried out the State's orders, and no one besides themselves (and old photographs from the year 2020) could perceive that they were anything other than State officials, part of the State fabric, and the fact that most of them voted in elections for the ruling party would hardly surprise anyone other than themselves, but they, on the other hand, would argue that they didn't want to throw away their own vote and by so doing bring the right-wingers into power. Nor were they being hypocritical. They just fundamentally did not conform in their own eyes, when all was said and done, to what they actually were.

Another of their distinctive traits was their relationship to the good things in life. They ate as became their position, resided likewise, had holiday homes and cars and boats and ever-increasing affluence, but it meant nothing, so they claimed, and rightly so. They had never dreamed of material wealth; in their dreams for the future, material wealth hadn't even been part of the scenario. Therefore they behaved as though these material goods were encumbrances in their lives. They didn't really concern them; they didn't define themselves through these objects which they enjoyed and which were there for one and all to see. This was particularly evident when one of them owned something that was extremely expensive or conspicuously striking, and that happened every so often, as they didn't deny themselves the good things in life. It would be explained as a personal deviation, and it was the person who owned the particularly expensive or striking object who themselves explained that it was a highly personal deviation. Per Ekeberg, for instance, owned a fast and extremely elegant car, and he explained this was due to him being possessed by a 'speed demon', which he never managed to banish, and Bernt Halvorsen had a large sailing boat lying at his fairly unpretentious holiday cottage in the county of Vestfold, and he apologised for this by saying that the wind and sailing held an almost abnormal attraction for him, which was connected to his childhood in a little town in Vestfold, the same one, by the way, that Professor Andersen had grown up in, without having to acquire a sailing boat when he was a grown man. Instead, Professor Andersen had another vice: a passion for Italian suits. In his wardrobe hung five light-weight woollen Italian suits, bought in Italy, it's true, while there on literary conferences, so they didn't cost more than an ordinary suit at home, he made a point of stressing – a whopping lie by the way. His Italian suits cost every bit as much as an Italian suit bought here at home; that is to say, if that suit could have been bought here at home at all, then it would have cost two or three thousand kroner more, so that, in a way, you could perhaps say that he had saved the price of one or two cheap Adelsten suits for every suit he bought in Italy. It wasn't often Professor Andersen wore one of these Italian suits, but what a delight it was for him when he did so once in a while. He seldom wore them when he had to be smart at a party, or when he had to represent the university or go to receptions, or quite simply when he gave a lecture. Tonight, for instance, he was wearing an ordinary, grey suit, the same one, by the way, that he had worn on Christmas Eve and Christmas Day, and on most days for everyday purposes he wore jeans. But now and then he had a great urge to get dressed up in one of his Italian suits, and then he did it, no matter what the occasion. Consequently, he could turn up at the university at Blindern dressed in one of his extremely elegant Italian suits made of pure wool. He delighted in turning up like that in front of his students, maybe just to lead a postgraduate seminar, or maybe even just a single tutorial with a postgraduate student in his office. He didn't do it to make an impression on his students, but to make an impression on himself. Getting dressed up in one of these suits gave him a heady, liberated feeling. Then he liked to go to a restaurant afterwards, alone, not an expensive restaurant either, and he delighted in dining absolutely alone at a small table by the window.

A non-materialistic dandy in an Italian suit alone at a table by the window in a restaurant. Fifty-five-year-old Professor Andersen, a representive of the small minority within his age group who could rightly claim to be a distinctive generation. Maybe the distinctive traits associated with their ways of acting and thinking could be traced back to a lifelong infatuation with the spirit of modernity, which had hit them and struck them down like lightning in their youth sometime in the Sixties. The avant-garde. The overriding futuristic alliance between political radicalism and the avant-garde in art. It was lodged deeply in their minds, as though still lightning-struck, like a lifelong infatuation. How much was left of their radicalism now was difficult to say. During the second referendum on whether Norway should enter the Common Market, which is now called the European Union, the seven people now gathered here were split more or less down the middle as regards how they cast their vote. Four of them had voted against, three had voted for, and who had voted one way or the other was relatively uninteresting, in Professor Andersen's opinion; what was interesting was that whether they had voted for or against, either way their vote was grounded in the spirit of their own youth or modernity. Professor Andersen himself had voted against, that was because he didn't see any reason to vote in favour, when most people living in all the far-flung corners of the country were so against; he didn't think he could quite defend going against farmers and fishermen and lorry drivers in thinly populated Norway, when it evidently meant so much to them that Norway shouldn't enter the European Union. Moreover, it pleased him to know that a number of ambitious young bureaucrats and politicians, several of whom he had tutored as students, missed out on a number of juicy positions within the EU bureaucracy, and they were really juicy positions, as regards both money and eminence; so when it was made known that the referendum result went against entering the EEC, then he thought about them in particular, especially the ones he actually knew and remembered as students, and he laughed, not so heartily as he had laughed the first time a referendum turned down entry into the EEC, in 1972 – no, much more heartily, in fact, much more crudely, for in 1972 he had been genuinely moved, as were many others. But Per Ekeberg had voted for entry, and he had made some condescending remarks about Professor Andersen's 'anti' standpoint, which he deemed rigid.

In order to understand these men and women who were

seated around a dinner table at Nina and Bernt Halvorsen's, the two married doctors, on this particular Boxing Day, then you have to understand Per Ekeberg and not least his self-assurance. For it was Per Ekeberg who was most loyal to the spirit of his youth. It might sound paradoxical, since he was the one who on the face of it had changed the most. He had made a complete break and left his senior position as a psychologist in the public sector for a position as director in an advertising agency which served large, commercial customers. It's true that he didn't use the title of Director, but continued to be called senior psychologist, a whim, or idea, which he had forced through, and which impressed people by turning out to be a highly creative idea in advertising terms, at the same time as it was a vehement expression of Per Ekeberg's own opinion of his new and, financially speaking, far more lucrative life. It was no fundamental change, in actual fact. He carried out the same duties as before, just in a new and more exciting setting. From being in state administration to being an agent in the open market, that was not a fundamental change. From being a social-democratic therapist to being a capitalistic player, that was not a fundamental change. This was an opinion which Per Ekeberg was able to uphold strongly and heatedly, just as he had upheld heatedly his views on any issue in which he had a consuming interest, ever since Professor Andersen had got to know him in the autumn of 1962. Per Ekeberg was the man of the future. That made him unflinchingly radical, he claimed, because it meant that he was able to consider without prejudice, and not least without old prestige, the new problems which arose, and Professor Andersen was by no means certain he wasn't right. Because their radicalism had perhaps only been a chance expression of the spirit of modernity, which was their one great fascination. So when Per Ekeberg was able to crow over Professor Andersen, telling him that it was he who was radical, and not Professor Andersen, who remained stuck in the out-dated ideas from his long-departed youth, then he did so with a self-assurance and deep sense of conviction that Professor Andersen himself didn't possess when he was trying to put forward his view, unsure of its radicalism. Because radicalism wasn't the issue, neither for Per Ekeberg nor for Professor Andersen. It was modernity. What gave the well-to-do advertising director his deep sense of conviction and (as far as Professor Andersen was concerned) crowing self-confidence wasn't the certainty that he, Per Ekeberg, was just as radical as he had always been, but that he was just as modern as he had always been. He claimed to be radical, but that was because his point of view was grounded in the modernity which had always influenced Per Ekeberg's life and work, and hence the standpoints of Professor Andersen and the other three who had voted against the EEC for the second time were stuffy and represented a decrepit radicalism. Professor Andersen found it difficult to defend himself against this, not because he happened to be against the EEC, but on account of what was associated with this standpoint, and which Per Ekeberg didn't have any trouble putting into words. Indeed, he had to admit that he envied Per Ekeberg his deep sense of conviction and pleasure at finding a shining modern policy for his own life. It wasn't Per Ekeberg crowing over his inability to adopt truly radical points of view that hurt him, because the hurt he felt on such occasions struck so deep that it had to be founded in nothing less than the fact that he perceived Per Ekeberg's accusation – about no longer being capable of adopting truly radical standpoints – as equivalent to accusing him of having lost the sense of modernity he had been infatuated with all his life, and which he had believed was an inalienable part of his character, and he felt stung by it. Faced with Per Ekeberg, Professor Andersen felt like a stuffy man in his fifties. He stuck to his standpoints, but he didn't like them, and would have liked to exchange them for more modern points of view if it had been possible for him to do so.

They sat around the dinner table. The starter had been consumed. The main course was being carried in. Grouse. Nina pointed out that the peas which accompanied the dish were Russian, and that it had been terribly difficult to get hold of them in this country. You see, there was actually only one single shop in the whole of Oslo where it was possible to get hold of Russian peas, and then you really ought to have ordered them in advance. Professor Andersen was then able to remark that he knew the shop Nina was referring to extremely well, he himself often purchased fish there, and then he had not infrequently heard other customers asking for Russian peas. He urged the others to guess which shop it might be. He did that to change the topic of conversation which had lasted throughout the starter, indeed right from the moment they were standing with an aperitif in their hands before the meal. What had happened was this; some days ago, just before Christmas, the very first programme by Judith Berg's daughter, Ingrid Guida, a new entertainment show called *Guida*, had been on TV, and on the NRK, the Norwegian Broadcasting Corporation, no less, so it was not surprising that it was subject to comment at this party, especially as one of the guests was the presenter's mother, and since the programme had received sensationally good reviews, it was natural to congratulate Judith Berg warmly, while they stood with their aperitifs in their hands. But this entertainment programme had also been discussed all through the starter, something that would have been fine in a way, if it weren't for the fact that only Per Ekeberg, Trine Napstad and Judith Berg had seen the programme; Professor Andersen hadn't seen it, Nina and Bernt hadn't seen it, and Jan Brynhildsen had also been prevented from seeing it, since he had been standing on the main stage of the National Theatre that evening; as a result they had ended up discussing an entertainment programme on TV which only a minority had seen and consequently could have an opinion on. But that did not trouble Per Ekeberg or Trine Napstad or Judith Berg. They had conducted an elated conversation about it, which the others more or less just had to follow, without contributing anything much. That was why Professor Andersen now attempted to steer the conversation towards something else by asking if the others could guess which shop it was in Oslo that was the only one that stocked Russian peas. Fjellberg, was the immediate reply from Jan Brynhildsen, and as a result the conversation about *Guida* resumed. For Trine Napstad had more to say about the entertainment programme on TV, as did Per Ekeberg too, of course, and Judith Berg wanted nothing more than to hear admiring comments about, and especially intelligent praise of, her daughter's success as a TV presenter. Now it wouldn't have been any trouble for Bernt Halvorsen, as the host, to lead the discussion on to another topic in a discreet manner, but he didn't. With a question for those of them who had seen it, from one who unfortunately hadn't seen it, he gave a hint to the rest of them who hadn't seen it that the conversation about this programme should continue, and that it was up to them to take part, using whatever means they had at their disposal. More than likely Bernt chose to do this as a token of consideration towards Judith. It was, after all, her big night, and it wasn't going to be spoiled by him, the host, disregarding her by signalling that they ought to talk about something else. Professor Andersen thought that Bernt probably had assumed it would be tactless. Perhaps his decision had also been reached following Judith's answer, when Trine Napstad had asked, responding to the fact that Jan Brynhildsen hadn't seen the programme because he was on stage when it was shown: 'But haven't you seen it on video afterwards?' Then Judith had said that she hadn't recorded it on video, 'because I think there are limits to how much interest I should show in my daughter's affairs'. Professor Andersen had liked that answer, and Bernt Halvorsen probably had, too; it showed great modesty and a sense of decency, despite being in a sphere where one wouldn't be observed by other people, apart from Jan Brynhildsen, her husband, that is. Obviously she was proud, her face glowed tonight, but nevertheless she had managed to fight back her urge to dwell on her daughter's success. From the admiring comments, congratulations and genuinely interested questions which Per Ekeberg and Trine Napstad put to Judith Berg about how the programme would be continued next Friday, Professor Andersen, and the other three who hadn't seen it, formed an impression of the kind of programme which had been so successful for Ingrid Guida, so that both he and the three others who hadn't seen it could take part in the conversation about it now and then, both with questions, comments and also astonished exclamations. *Guida* was a programme that centred around the 23-year-old presenter's personality, and celebrities from the fields of Norwegian politics, finance, culture and entertainment were her guests, bowing and scraping to her, allowing themselves to be depicted as walk-on characters in staged and bizarre episodes. She persuaded priests in sequins to dance behind her up the aisle in Oslo Cathedral, for instance, or doctors along the hospital corridors. She was the seducer who got the pillars of society to break out of their roles and profane them. She coaxed ministers of State to dress up in costumes making fun of themselves, and to strike poses which everyone would have thought embarrassing for them, if it wasn't for the fact that they let themselves be stage-directed into them, something that led Professor Andersen, who hadn't seen the programme, to exclaim: 'But then they must lose their sting, surely,' while Bernt Halvorsen, in response to almost everything *he* heard, exclaimed: 'No, that surely isn't possible,' which made Per Ekeberg, Trine Napstad or Judith Berg laugh and relish the situation, as they had seen the programme and could assure them that it really was possible, yes, everything was possible, even though Bernt Halvorsen with his 'No, that surely isn't possible' had only meant to be polite and obliging, and was certainly not expressing his intensely curious incredulity towards a programme he hadn't seen, and probably didn't intend to see next Friday either, while in response to Professor Andersen's outburst Per Ekeberg retorted sharply: 'This has nothing to do with sting, it is displaying a lifestyle.'

By that time they had almost finished their grouse, served with a delicious savoury sauce, and the aforementioned Russian peas. And at this point in the meal Nina, their hostess, disclosed to the dinner party that she now had begun to wonder if it hadn't been a mistake to serve Rioja with the grouse, after all. Though, for that matter, it couldn't have been totally wrong, but maybe it would have been better with a burgundy. But no, on the other hand, a good burgundy costs so much that it would almost seem a bit ostentatious to serve it, wouldn't it, and as for the cheap wines, are they really so good that they . . . well, anyway, here we are drinking Rioja at any rate, and it's too late to regret it. Skol, she laughed, and everybody skolled with her and assured her that the Rioja was quite excellent, and definitely better than serving a mediocre burgundy with the grouse. Jan Brynhildsen told them an amusing tale about why the State Wine Monopoly had to change its old logo, which was pretty similar to King Olav V's insignia (V in Vinmonopol and V in King Olav V), and that prompted Per Ekeberg to tell an equally amusing tale about why it had altered the label on the popular cheap, house red wine, which in previous years had had a drawing of the bridges over the Seine in Paris, right until Sonja became Queen of Norway. Bernt talked eagerly, partly assisted, partly contra-dicted by Nina, about how Christmas Eve had passed in their home this year, with pork ribs, lutefisk, electricity cuts and twelve people in all, counting children and adults, with hard-of-hearing grandparents from Bernt's side of the family and half-blind ones from Nina's side, recounted in a typically doctorly fashion, by both Bernt and his partly reluctant Nina. The atmosphere was loosening up, and Professor Andersen sneaked a discreet glance at his watch. Cloudberry cream for dessert. The cloudberries, too, were from Valdres, where Nina and Bernt had a cottage in the mountains. Trine Napstad was in a lively mood, and her piercing voice contrasted well, and rather mercilessly, with Professor Andersen's eternal deep rumblings, or so he thought. He really would have liked to rise to the occasion, to the same level of bonhomie and cheerfulness, but despite assiduous efforts it was beyond him. After the dessert they continued to sit at the round dinner table, drinking wine. Professor Andersen wished they would move over to the sofa, as then it would have been easier to leave without one having to think there would be a great, gaping hole at the table. But the coffee, too, was served at the round table. A small glass of cognac. Bernt uncorked another few bottles of wine, and put them on the table, where he had also placed the bottle of cognac in case anyone wanted to drink cognac rather than wine from now on. Professor Andersen looked at his watch. Gone eleven. He was amazed it was so late already, because he desperately longed to go home. He had to go home now, before night fell. He went to the toilet to gather his thoughts. When he returned to the others, he said, addressing Nina and Bernt, that he thought he had to leave now. The other guests looked at him in surprise, but not Nina and Bernt. He said that he had been feeling slightly unwell all day, he wondered if he was about to get a bout of the flu, and he asked Bernt to phone for a taxi. Bernt got up and went to the phone. He nodded goodbye to Jan Brynhildsen and Judith Berg, to Per Ekeberg and Trine Napstad, and went into the hall, followed by Nina. He put on his overcoat and apologised to her for having to leave so early, before Bernt came out and said the taxi was on its way, and he apologised once again. 'Perhaps it isn't even influenza,' he said, 'perhaps I'm just worn out by my own thoughts. I've been thinking so much recently, about literature and how time breaks it down, perhaps they are new thoughts, but at any rate they are heavy,' he said. They said that they understood, it was nothing to worry about, of course one should leave early if one was weighed down by heavy thoughts. Oh, he felt so indescribably sad at heart, face to face with Nina and Bernt, because he didn't have the peace of mind to stay there any longer now that it was just past eleven. Indeed, he felt dispirited by his own behaviour. Through the glass in the outside door he could see the taxi arriving and stopping in front of the driveway. Professor Andersen opened the door and went out to the waiting car, and sat down in the back seat, while he waved to his hosts, who were standing in the doorway waving back.

He gave the address to the driver, who drove him through the snowy streets of Oslo all lit up with Christmas lights. It had stopped snowing, but the road conditions were terrible. The taxi drove slowly through the streets, which were impassable except by means of two deep tyre tracks down the middle, and on meeting another car, one of them had to reverse. But he could observe snowploughs every-where and other snow-clearing vehicles, which were working flat out with loops of yellow lights in all directions. They gave off a roar. The driver was from Pakistan and drove safely and carefully through the almost snowbound but lamplit streets. There were few people to be seen, even in the main streets which they crossed, such as Bogstadveien. Professor Andersen was sitting in the back seat, feeling tense. He couldn't get home soon enough. Eventually, the taxi drew up at the building where he lived at Skillebekk, and he paid and got out. He quickly unlocked the main door, went up the stairs and let himself into his own apartment, where he put on the light in the hall and hung up his overcoat. Then he went into the living room, without putting on the light, where he moved over to the window and stared across at the building on the other side of the street. The curtains were drawn back. The light was on. Finally! Now he would be able to see. Professor Andersen stood in the pitch dark in his own living room, half-hidden behind the curtain, and stared out. He noticed a figure walking through the room. Professor Andersen stared as hard as he could, but the whole thing happened so fast that he couldn't quite grasp what he had seen, even though the figure hadn't walked particularly quickly through the room. He thought it was a man, but he wasn't absolutely certain. Professor Andersen waited. The silhouette had disappeared, probably sitting somewhere out of sight, but Professor Andersen waited. Eventually the silhouette turned up again. The figure walked through the lit-up room and went over now towards the window. A face stared out and Professor Andersen saw the murderer's face. Not all that clearly, not to the extent that he would have been able to recognise the person on the street later on, but he saw that it was a youngish man.

Was he disappointed? Had he hoped that the figure which passed through the room had been a woman after all, and that the young woman with fair hair would be standing at the window now? Professor Andersen didn't know. If he had been hoping this, and it had been keeping him glued to this window, and to this view, both in reality and in his thoughts, then his hope had been unrealistic and actually a prayer for a miracle. Or rather a prayer that he, Professor Andersen, might not be able to trust his own senses, his own eyes, in decisive situations, and that what he thought he saw might equally well be a fantasy or a hallucination, had he cherished such a hope? Even, when all is said and done, if it meant his reason was threatened? Or was what he saw now exactly what he had hoped to see: the murderer's face? Professor Andersen didn't know, and suddenly he started to cry, not with tears, but with words. 'I'm crying,' he said, and gave himself over to this simple sentence, which he repeated several times while he stood at the window, long after the youngish man in the other window had turned away, walked through the room and retreated out of sight, to somewhere from which he didn't reappear.

The next day was the day after Boxing Day, a working day, shops and offices, banks and post offices were open. Professor Andersen decided to go away for a while. He packed a small suitcase and took a taxi out to Fornebu Airport, where he checked in on the first plane to Trondheim. He phoned the Britannia Hotel and booked a room. Then he called one of his colleagues and said that he was going to be in Trondheim over the New Year, and they arranged to meet the next day. On the plane trip up there it was so overcast that he couldn't see a thing. From Værnes he took the airport bus to the Britannia Hotel and checked in. On the flight he had ploughed through the newspapers and, as he expected, found nothing about the murder he had witnessed. Now he ploughed through them again. Nothing. No woman reported missing, for instance, who could be connected to what he had witnessed. He went outside and strolled around the streets of Trondheim. The man's name was Henrik Nordstrøm. He had found that out before deciding to go to Trondheim. He had gone across the street and stopped in front of the main door of the building, and had found out which nameplate and doorbell must belong to the apartment where he had seen the murderer's face the evening before. As ever when he visited Trondheim, he went into the late-twelfth-century cathedral, the only thing from the Norwegian Middle Ages that bears witness to a sophisticated culture. He also popped into Erichsen's coffee shop and had a cup of coffee and a piece of cake; that, too, was a habit of his. While he was walking around the streets, he suddenly bumped into his colleague's ex-wife, with whom he had to pass the time of day, as it was too late to pretend he hadn't noticed her. He didn't mention that he was going to meet her ex-husband the next day. When he came back to the Britannia, a man who had been sitting in the foyer got to his feet and came towards him. It was his colleague. He would really like to meet him at once, today, he said, since he didn't have anything special on. That pleased Professor Andersen and he invited his colleague up to his room.

He told his colleague to take a seat in an armchair, while he fetched a bottle of whisky, which he had wisely just bought at the Wine Monopoly in Kjøpmannsgata in Trondheim. He got hold of ice cubes and Farris mineral water from the mini-bar, while he went on about how one had to be careful that it was blue Farris one had, and not yellow. Once, it was at Hoyer's Hotel in Skien, he had just taken Farris without thinking any more about it, and his whisky had a taste of lemon. 'Bloody hell! And the worst of it was,' said Professor Andersen as he put two empty glasses, blue Farris and a glass of ice cubes on the table, 'there was just yellow Farris in the mini-bar. What a hotel!' 'That's so the guests don't sit in their rooms drinking whisky, but go down to the bar and buy it there,' said his colleague. 'Yes, of course, but still, it's not particularly agreeable.' They both poured themselves a whisky and skolled their unexpected encounter. When Professor Andersen saw that his colleague was sitting there, dying to know what on earth had brought him to Trondheim in the Christmas period, he decided to come straight to the point. 'Have you ever thought,' he said, 'how short a historical memory we have? Can you remember your own grandparents?' 'Yes, of course,' said his colleague, surprised, 'I remember them well.' 'I do, too,' said Professor Andersen, 'even though both my grandparents were dead when I was born. But I've heard so much about them that for that reason I can say, historically speaking, that I know them. But what about your great-grandparents?' His colleague went quiet; he was thinking about it. 'You know, I don't know much about them.' 'You do have *eight* great-grandparents,' said Professor Andersen with emphasis on the words. 'And there is probably barely a hundred years between the birth of the eldest of them and you. And already they're no longer part of your consciousness. Indeed, even worse, they've never existed in your consciousness.' His colleague looked rather taken aback. 'It isn't as bad as all that,' he said, after he had thought about it. 'I do know something. I've even seen one of them in a photograph. He was a shoemaker in Fredrikstad.' 'And where is that photograph now?' 'Ah, I don't know that.' 'And you call that knowing something about your great-grandparents?' His colleague looked a little taken aback again. 'You're right,' he said. 'It's peculiar, and I've never even thought about it before.' 'It's more than peculiar,' said Professor Andersen, 'it's embarrassing. Perhaps even frightening. Here we are, the two of us, sitting in a hotel room in Trondheim around Christmas, and the light of our consciousness doesn't reach back more than two generations. After that it begins to fade, a twilight memory here, a photograph no one knows the whereabouts of there. Then it's dark. And we are both professors of literature.' 'Yes, indeed, of literature. We aren't historians,' said his colleague, defending himself. 'Besides, we do have another kind of recollection which goes much further than our ties of kinship, we remember things with a connection to our work, in our case within the field of literature. You know many tales about Ludvig Daae, too, don't you? Or you can conjure up the memory of Lorentz Dietrichsson, indeed, maybe even Jonas Collett?' his colleague said triumphantly. 'You're right about that. But these eight great-grandparents of yours have nevertheless given you your genes; barely sixty or seventy years ago they were young and passed on their genes to the person who in turn bred the person who gave you your genes, and you have no recollection of them – isn't it . . . ?' 'Well, yes, peculiar. Not embarrassing. And not frightening,' his colleague broke in. 'I find it frightening,' continued Professor Andersen, unremittingly. 'What does it mean? Is it some-thing common to humans, in other words a human trait, as living creatures, which we haven't bothered to register, because the fact that humans are historical beings is so commonplace that it can't be challenged? Or is it a charac-teristic of humanity in the present day, and in our cultural circle? Or does it only apply to us who come from the common people? I don't know, but it has something to do with our day and age, that's for sure. There is something about it which makes us not particularly interested in what has gone before us, at any rate much less than we pretend is the case. It has something to do with being modern. And it must have begun early on, for both of us would have known about our great-grandparents if our parents had any interest in telling us about them, but evidently they didn't; it isn't that they quite simply forgot them, I don't believe that. Our down-to-earth parents, these stuffy people, with their enthusiasm for plastic and the weather forecasts on the radio, must, in that case, have been bearers of a fundamental modernity, which they've passed on to us, without anyone being aware of it even. This has only dawned on me quite recently. The fact that my enlightened consciousness goes back no further than two generations, then it's dark.' 'But now I must be allowed to interrupt you a moment,' said his colleague eagerly, 'because with regard to what you're saying, I can only answer that there are few countries where you'll find so great an interest in history as in our country, particularly history at the grass-roots level. Remember, every single town or small village has its own local history book, usually in three volumes. And every generation would like to write a new one, right from scratch and in three volumes. So don't give me that. Or take the enormous interest there is in genealogy in this country. Or all the kinship gatherings at which people assemble every summer.' 'Well, well, that's true. But nonetheless it doesn't apply to either of us, and we are, after all, professors of literature. *Our* common social consciousness isn't influenced by these cranky genealogists or local historians. Praiseworthy though they may be, these cranks who sit beside us in the University Library pursuing the traces of their own origins down through the ages, though they ought to give us hope, because they demonstrate that it is possible to break out of this common consciousness and go one's own way, if only one's passion and personal determination are great enough, they are and remain cranks who fail to leave any mark on the common consciousness, no matter how sympathetic our attitude may be to their pursuits, and not least to the intentions behind them. They are and will continue to be total outsiders. They do not affect us, our very structure and sensibility, which form the way we think. Indeed, it frightens me,' he repeated. 'It really frightens me. It frightens me much more than the fact that I'm childless.' Then he held his tongue, and remained sitting in silence. His colleague didn't say anything either. He looked at Professor Andersen, he seemed to be about to say something, he drew himself up the way someone does who is going to say something he must or ought to say, but is uncertain if he will after all, but he finally decided not to say anything, and remained seated, looking, rather puzzled, at Professor Andersen.

It went quiet for a while. The two men drank whisky in Professor Andersen's room at the Britannia Hotel. To tell the truth, they drank a lot; the bottle was close to being half empty. It was no later than 3 p.m. Outside the window it had already begun to get dark. Professor Andersen's colleague was a few years younger than him, approaching fifty, though he hadn't reached it yet. He had just started a new life, in so far as he had got married a second time, to a young woman, one of his students no less. This Professor Andersen knew, but he hadn't touched on it as yet, and his colleague hadn't had an opportunity to do so himself, as Professor Andersen had started talking straight away about what was on his mind, and which, after all, was the reason why he had phoned his colleague from Fornebu when it suddenly occurred to him to go up to Trondheim. He poured yet another whisky for himself and handed the bottle to the other man, while he was thinking that he must try to continue with his deliberations before he became so intoxicated that he couldn't continue, but would just repeat himself, over and over again, using exactly the same words, as he knew he had a habit of doing under the influence of alcohol.

'Recently I've begun to look at myself in a different light than I did before,' continued Professor Andersen. 'Previously I regarded myself as a person who was able to use my resources to the full, and was, to be perfectly honest, proud of that ability. Now I see clearly how limited my horizon is, and it surprises me that I haven't seen it before. Imagine how I've gone round calling myself enlightened and aware, even claiming to have an understanding of history, and actually I haven't any knowledge of my ancestors even three generations back, and worse still: I've not even been concerned about this. It is utterly disgraceful,' he shouted, and thumped his fist on the table-top, so that the blue Farris (the second one) overturned, and the whisky splashed over his glass. 'This is the state of the human spirit in our time,' he continued, after drying the table-top with his handkerchief. 'Of which we are both outstanding and excellent representatives. There is something primitive about it which we haven't been able to face up to. I'm scared,' he said, 'and frightened by my own ignorance. I've reached the age of fifty-five, and am not eager to throw myself into a new field of study.' He went silent. 'But if that is the case,' his colleague said eagerly, 'then what you say is surely an unusually weighty defence as to the necessity of art and literature.' 'Oh, don't be so sure about that,' said Professor Andersen with a fierce smile, which he reckoned he would have characterised as evil if he had seen himself from outside.

He felt quite inebriated, so he decided not to continue this conversation. He asked his colleague how he was, and the latter immediately began to talk about his affairs. The contents of the whisky bottle became dangerously low, and Professor Andersen was obliged to call room service and order two more bottles of blue Farris, as well as a bucket of ice. It can't be denied that Professor Andersen listened with only half an ear (of altogether two whole ones) to what his colleague told him about his affairs. For his part, his colleague was still clearly preoccupied with what had brought Professor Andersen to Trondheim over the Christmas period, and when he heard that there wasn't any particular reason for it, and that he didn't have any particular plans for the next few days either, he immediately invited Professor Andersen to stay with him, an offer Professor Andersen emphatically declined. He preferred, in fact, to stay at a hotel when he was out travelling. 'Yes, if you can afford it,' said his colleague, possibly slightly offended. 'I treat myself,' answered Professor Andersen, and he noticed that he was proud of being able to say that he treated himself to staying in a hotel when he was out travelling. His colleague got up and made a phone call. Professor Andersen understood that he was phoning home to his young wife, for he heard him say that he was bringing a guest home for dinner. He also heard sounds which could be interpreted as protests on the other end of the line, and his colleague said: 'It'll be fine,' before he put down the receiver and, beaming, invited Professor Andersen to dinner. A little later the whisky bottle was empty, and the two gentlemen left the Britannia Hotel in an excessively good mood.

Outside on the street his colleague pointed at a car parked by the kerb, and said, 'That's my car. I had no idea I'd be drinking in the afternoon.' They walked along the street. Professor Andersen asked where they were headed. 'Home to my place,' said his colleague. 'We have to get a bus as it's too far to walk.' 'Can't we take a taxi, then?' asked Professor Andersen. 'Taxi?' said his colleague. 'Yes indeed, we can take a taxi. I hadn't thought of that.' So they hailed a taxi, and a little later they came to a stop outside a house on a hillside above the centre of Trondheim.

Professor Andersen paid for the taxi and they got out and went into the house. There his colleague's young wife was standing, holding a small child in her arms. She breastfed it, unselfconsciously and openly. She said that they only had fishcakes for dinner. Professor Andersen said that he looked forward to eating fishcakes, especially in Trondheim, where they really could make fishcakes. The young wife and mother replied that they were ready-made fishcakes, the kind you could buy in every supermarket in the country, but Professor Andersen said he looked forward to them, nonetheless. He asked what the child was called, and told them an anecdote from the University of Oslo, which his colleague, as well as his young wife, thought highly amusing. 'Well, as you can see, I've begun on a second brood,' said his colleague to Professor Andersen when his young wife was out in the kitchen preparing the fishcakes. 'She's still studying,' he added. The dinner was splendid. Indeed, Professor Andersen enjoyed sitting like that in the kitchen in a private home eating ready-made fishcakes with boiled potatoes and grated carrots. With a brown sauce. And fried onions. The only thing he was slightly dissatisfied with was that there was only half a bottle of beer to share between them with the meal; that was rather little for him, with the alcohol still going to his head. But after the meal they had coffee, and then his colleague got out a bottle. 'This isn't exactly whisky or French cognac,' he said, 'but something much better. A drink popular in Trøndelag: karsk.' He poured this into the coffee. They stirred it and drank. 'Skol for your child,' said Professor Andersen, and both his colleague and his young wife nodded in a friendly way, and smiled happily and skolled in return and thanked him; the young mother didn't have karsk in her coffee, it's true, but she skolled and thanked him, nonetheless. His colleague said it was terribly nice that Professor Andersen had chosen to spend the Christmas week and New Year's Eve in Trondheim, and his young wife agreed. They immediately invited Professor Andersen to a New Year's Eve party. Not in their own home, but with some friends of theirs, and when Professor Andersen protested and said that it might well be inconvenient, his colleague got up and phoned the friends they were going to visit, and said that he would like to bring along another guest, Professor Andersen from the University of Oslo, and when he put down the phone, he said that they would be pleased if Pål Andersen came along. Tomorrow he wanted to go skiing with Andersen. But Professor Andersen didn't have any skiing equipment with him. 'We'll fix that,' said his colleague and went down into the cellar and brought up a pair of old skis. Professor Andersen had to try skis and ski-poles, boots and bindings, and his colleague didn't give up until everything fitted. He borrowed an anorak and knickerbockers as well, his colleague's discarded ones; not exactly the latest fashion, but he hadn't come to Trondheim to look stunning on the ski slope, had he, ha ha. His colleague's young wife sat down with her sewing things and measured up and sewed in the anorak and the knickerbockers, so they wouldn't hang off him, flapping around, as his colleague was a good deal stouter than Professor Andersen. In high spirits, even though it was quite early, Professor Andersen said goodbye to his colleague and his wife. Back at the hotel he ransacked the mini-bar looking for a drink, before he recollected that in Nordic hotels there aren't any drinks in the mini-bar, just wine and beer. He called room service for a double whisky and soda. He had to have something to send him to sleep, and also to get rid of the reek of karsk which still lingered, even though he had drunk as little of it as possible.

The next morning Professor Andersen and his colleague from Trondheim went skiing. His colleague drove out to a place called Bymarka, which was a popular skiing area. They took the skis and poles down from the roof rack and, standing next to the car, started to rub on wax. It was really miserable, chilly weather. Overcast, rather cold, and with snow and drizzle in the air. His colleague took the business of selecting ski wax very seriously. He had a thermometer with him, which he stuck in the snow to measure the temperature, then suggested to Professor Andersen that they should choose green wax as an under-coat, and blue wax on top of that, which Professor Andersen agreed with. He informed his colleague at the same time that, though it was true that he, like all Norwegians, was born with skis on his feet, nevertheless it was a long time ago, so he suggested they should go on a nice easy ski trip, something his colleague didn't object to. With nice, easy strokes they set off through Bymarka in Trondheim. When they came to a downhill slope, his colleague set out boldly and confidently, while Professor Andersen stood a moment at the top and surveyed the situation, before he, too, set off. On the uphill slopes his colleague demonstrated his agility, and rushed upwards on light skis, while Professor

Andersen again took it nice and easy and moved at his own pace. But over the flattish stretches they went side by side. After a while they arrived at a skiers' cabin, where they went in and each had a hot blackcurrant drink. Professor Andersen took the opportunity, as he had done yesterday, to talk about something that was weighing on his mind. He was anxious about the future. His own future, as a professor of literature. Literature is not going to survive, not in the way we think of it. Its survival is just a matter of form, and that is no longer enough. All enthusiasm lies in the present, and in our day and age nothing can outdo the ability of commercialism to arouse enthusiasm and stir the hearts of the masses, and that is the spirit of the present time. He was afraid they had suffered a definitive defeat. They had to look this fact in the eye, if for no other reason than for their own peace of mind. He, for his part, couldn't share the enthusiasm felt by the masses for the token forms of culture they were being offered; he didn't understand how one could possibly feel enthusiastic about such things, but in practice it was quite evident that he erred, at any rate with regard to that. He didn't want to comment on the quality of such culture, at least not to his colleague, who could see this too. He no longer wanted to conceal the fact that he thought the time he lived in was pathetic. He didn't enjoy living in it at all, but at the same time he couldn't present an alternative to it. 'Because we aren't timeless intellectuals, we are intellectuals in a commercial age, and deeply influenced by what stirs the hearts of the

masses. What stirs the hearts of the masses are the consequences of our own inadequacy. Purely and simply. When
were you last strongly stirred by watching or reading a
Greek tragedy? I mean really stirred, shaken to the depths
of your being. Not just nodding in recognition, quietly
enjoying it, which we ought not to underestimate, that has
to be said, quiet enjoyment has its significance, for the two
of us. But stirred. As you can be when reading a novel from
our own day and age? I think I'm on to something here.
Our relationship to the past is marked by deep indifference,
even if we do say something to the contrary, and even if
we mean what we say when we say that it's a matter of the
greatest significance. Because it is a matter of the greatest
significance, yet nevertheless we feel so bound to it by a
sense of duty. It looks like our consciousness is insufficiently
equipped to fulfil the body's need for spiritual immortality.
I can say that, being a professor of literature, and say it to
you, my colleague. My nerves shriek in dread at the thought
of no longer possessing a historical consciousness, because
it means that our day and age will disappear along with
us, so when we stage Ibsen at the National Theatre, my
nerves relax, because if we can stage a play from the last
century in one of the country's finest buildings, with exten-
sive publicity and often to a full house, then the coming
generations may regard us in the same light. But it isn't
Ibsen's work we perform, it's Ibsen's reputation. To the
work as such, we are more or less indifferent, yes we are,
now barely a hundred years after it was written. It's the

stage director's work we see performed, Stein Winge's or Kjetil Bang Hansen's. It's Winge's work and Ibsen's reputation. My stomach churns in protest at the thought of there being no reputation so great that it can't survive a hundred years. We want to have immortal works, but do such things exist, for us? Ibsen's best plays are just barely a hundred years old, we call them immortal already, but are they? Even now we can see how difficult it is to make them seem relevant to us. On stage they have to be modernised and made contemporary, so that we will experience something so-called great while watching them, and even then it doesn't succeed, as a rule. And as drama to be read? Occasionally I think, after having read through and studied, for instance, *Ghosts*: well, was that all? Was there nothing else? Was this the most outstanding accomplishment of the 1880s, was this the most outstanding intellectual accomplishment in Europe in the nineteenth century? Certainly it's good, but is it really the most outstanding achievement that can be accomplished? It will probably turn out that it is, but my question still remains: was that all? Is there nothing else? I have actually studied *Ghosts* for years, and know that it's perfect. Yes I am and will continue to be impressed by what it is, perfect, but nonetheless I ask: was that all? Was that it? I am not stirred by it. I'm not shaken. Not like the audience when it was performed for the first time, as a contemporary event. In my case it has not survived as the actual revelation it once was, and so how can I carry out my duty to society, which is to pass this play down to new generations? I'm in doubt, I'm so terribly in doubt about my own function in this age, which I really cannot stand any longer. The ravages of time, that is what gnaws at me, destroying everything. The ravages of time gnaw at even the most outstanding intellectual accomplishments and destroy them, making them pale and faded.' 'But you must be able to accept the patina of time,' his colleague said suddenly.

His colleague had been sitting, listening calmly to Professor Andersen's outpourings, because he probably understood that they came from the heart, and therefore didn't interrupt him. But now he could no longer hold his tongue, and a discussion arose between the two gentlemen about the patina of time. A discussion about the upheavals versus the quiet enjoyment afforded by art, and about whether it wasn't their task as professors of literature to pass on this quiet enjoyment, and not the stirring aspects, to their students. His colleague strongly maintained that it was their task to convey a sense of quiet enjoyment, and not stirring emotions, which in any case, as Professor Andersen so rightly pointed out, had been lost long ago in the historic moments from which the work of art had once sprung. The essential thing to recognise, and enjoy, was the noble patina which rested on a work of art which had lasted beyond its own century. 'That is also historical aware-ness. Nothing else is in our power, and that is enough,' maintained his colleague. 'That is answer enough with regard to our deep desire to have something that outlasts us.' He wasn't stirred by reading Dante's *The Divine Comedy*, not even by its depictions of Hell, and it wasn't something he missed. But he could quietly and genuinely enjoy reading this work written in Florence in the thirteenth century, both because it actually was accessible to him, a Norwegian at the end of the twentieth century, and because the conditions both he and Professor Andersen endured in life, when all was said and done, were such that it was possible for him, after painstaking study, to relate to the work itself, yes, even to understand it. That the freshness was gone wasn't something he missed, the noble weight bestowed by the patina fully compensated for that. Professor Andersen maintained in reply that his colleague probably didn't fully understand what he was attempting to say, nor to what extent it troubled him. He certainly didn't underrate the noble patina, he merely wanted to point out the consequences of the fact that there is no great stir in the modern sense when studying and gaining insight into a canonical work, consequences which Professor Andersen suspected might be approaching the dreadful consequences that spring out of breaking a taboo, or tampering with one. The silent despair of someone who does something like that. Indeed, he had to be allowed to express himself in this way, even if it didn't sound sufficiently stringent to his colleague, because the thoughts he had were rather vague, but were no less troublesome on that account. He was obliged to question whether the quiet enjoyment his colleague talked about was an expression of perplexity with regard to history, and our true relationship to it. That there is an element of resignation involved, that he fully understood and respected, indeed, he dared also say, shared; even so it alleviated an unease he was no longer capable of alleviating. The suspicion that human consciousness was not sufficient to create works of art fit to survive their own period. The futile battle of consciousness against time. 'The patina is necessary to cover up this horrifying state of affairs, that is what I am afraid of,' said Professor Andersen. 'We have such a burning desire for something we are incapable of achieving, and we can't bear to face up to this lack of ability. We can't, because that will drown our consciousness, and with it human dignity. One may find the meaninglessness great enough as it is, even in a world which believes in immortality through great intellectual accomplishments which survive the ravages of time. Which the ravages of time do not affect. Oh, what a marvellous thought, what a pleasing concept that expresses. Indeed, perhaps we can compare this to our own individual lives and the bright expectations we have about our experiences. All of us would like to become wiser individuals as the years pass, but is it true that we do? In my case it definitely isn't. I'm not a wiser person now than when I was twenty-five years old, I'm just older. The experiences I've had aren't worth much to anyone but myself. My experiences are of no value so they can be passed on to others, and younger individuals; they are a burden I have to bear alone. I have to relate to my experiences, mainly as impediments that make me mindful of my age, so I don't continue to act "youthful", "young in spirit", something which is distasteful, if I may say so.' 'Now I'm beginning to understand a little of what you mean,' his colleague interjected. 'And everything is pretty black, really. You cast doubt on everything you can cast doubt on, and I must simply admit my situation in life is not such that there is any attraction in letting myself be tempted by your points of view. No, Pål, old chap, if we want to get down to the car before it gets dark, we'll just have to get a move on.'

They stood up. They had been sitting in the crowded ski cabin for several hours. It had already begun to grow dark outside, the daylight hours are so short up here in the north in December. They had a place at a large table for six at first, but moved over to a table for two when it became vacant. Throughout the tirades and the discussion which arose, Professor Andersen had got up twice and stood in the queue to buy them coffee; on one occasion he had also brought a plate with two Danish pastries back to the table. New skiers kept coming into the ski cabin, bringing with them a whiff of fresh snow and wind into the packed, slightly clammy premises. There was the tramp of boots, the smell of ski wax, and of caps and mittens and scarfs. However, when Professor Andersen and his colleague got up and left, it was beginning to thin out.

They fastened their skis on and took hold of their ski poles. His colleague sped off down the slope, in the tracks between the silver-grey and gloomy fir trees, and came to a halt down there to wait for Professor Andersen, who was still standing at the top and taking his time. He calculated his own route down with as long and wide turns as possible, before setting off downhill and completing the downhill slopes in accordance with his calculations, wobbling downwards without falling, and not without a certain inherited mastery over his skis, unfit though he was. At the bottom his colleague was still waiting, and they continued together across the open, gently sloping ground, his colleague first and Professor Andersen after him, a little out of breath, despite the fact that his colleague went at as slow a pace as possible. It got darker and darker before they could catch a glimpse of the lit car park in the distance. Then his colleague said that he would like to speed up a little on the last part, and set off, agilely, while Professor Andersen continued at the same pace, perhaps a little slower. When he reached the car, his colleague had already fastened his skis on to the roof rack and stood stretching out. He said that now it would be good to come home to dinner, in a tone which made Professor Andersen wonder if he didn't expect Professor Andersen to join him. So he mentioned in passing that he intended to eat dinner alone at the hotel today. His colleague protested energetically. 'But Mette has been making food all day!' he exclaimed. 'She has really been looking forward to serving you genuine Trøndelag sodd. You can't turn that down now!' Professor Andersen realised this, and sat in the passenger seat beside his colleague and went home with him for dinner.

His young wife, Mette, was sitting in the living room

breast-feeding their child. She gave them a friendly smile. Afterwards, she carried the child into the bedroom so that it could sleep. They sat down at the table. His colleague opened a bottle of lager, which he poured out for Professor Andersen and himself. 'Oh, there's nothing like coming home to lovely hot sodd after a good long ski-trip!' he exclaimed, with a sigh of satisfaction. Professor Andersen said he agreed. Mette smiled and said she thought she ought to make it, since he got ready-made fishcakes yesterday. She couldn't put the cathedral city to shame, as she said. After the meal they had coffee, and Professor Andersen was obliged to have a drop of karsk in his cup again. The atmosphere was cosy, and Professor Andersen thought he had to do something in return. Therefore, he invited them out to dinner the next evening. At Palmehaven, the high-class restaurant at the Britannia Hotel. He saw that Mette was glad to be invited out, for she immediately began to discuss getting a babysitter with her husband. They sat talking about this, that and the other, until Professor Andersen stood up early in the evening and said that now he had to get back to the hotel. He asked his colleague to phone for a taxi. Back at the hotel he called room service for a double whisky and soda, and afterwards took a stroll around the town. He popped into a restaurant where there were a number of people and had a beer there, before he walked back to the hotel again and went to bed early, after a short visit to the bar.

In the morning he woke up very early, in the pitch-dark.

'Henrik Nordstrøm.' The name. It didn't have to be him. The man in the window didn't have to be Henrik Nordstrøm. Henrik Nordstrøm was just the name that was on the doorbell which belonged to the apartment where he had seen a murder being committed. It could have been rented out to another person, for a long or a short period of time, most likely short, since Henrik Nordstrøm's name was still there on its own without anyone else's taped over it. Or it could have been lent out to a friend at Christmas, either by Henrik Nordstrøm or by his possible tenants. Or even worse: the tenant was a woman, the woman he had seen standing at the window just before midnight on the night before Christmas Day. Professor Andersen turned cold inside. He got up straight away, turned on the light, looked at his watch. Half past six. He had to get back to Oslo immediately. He mustn't lose him. What if he had disappeared already? He called reception to request them to make up the bill. Got ready to leave. He was in a daze. He felt that he might have made an irreversible blunder going off in the way he had done. Down at reception he asked the man behind the desk to phone the airport and book a seat on the first plane available. That was done, and soon after Professor Andersen was sitting in the back seat of a taxi on his way out to Værnes Airport.

At Værnes he managed to phone his colleague and apologise, saying that he unfortunately had to leave for Oslo, for he had received a message which meant that he had to return straight away. Where he came from, he added to himself. On the plane he ploughed through the newspapers. Nothing. There was nothing outside the windows either. Thick mist. Grey. White. His eyes smarted from looking out and down. The plane lurched due to air turbulence. Rough Norwegian weather. He couldn't avoid having a guilty conscience. Towards his colleague and his young wife. He had, after all, invited them to dinner at Palmehaven tonight. They had been looking forward to it, and he had been looking forward to it himself because they, especially the young wife, Mette, so evidently and candidly had been looking forward to it. He recollected that he hadn't even cancelled the table he had reserved yesterday evening, a table for three at Palmehaven. But he would have to do that when he arrived in Oslo. He felt a bit sorry for his colleague, who probably didn't have much cash, starting a second family had its costs, even for a professor of literature, especially when the possessions of one's former life were to be divided in two, and not a penny less, he reckoned, bearing in mind what he knew about his colleague's ex-wife. It had therefore been something for them to look forward to, having dinner with the lavish colleague from Oslo (Professor Andersen). They had fixed up a babysitter, too, and then he, Professor Andersen, had just done a runner from the whole thing. It wasn't on. No, it wasn't on.

In the taxi from Fornebu Airport to Skillebekk he tried to calm himself down, but couldn't. He was too tense. He hastily opened the main door of the building where he lived, and went quickly up the stairs and unlocked the door to his apartment. He went straight over to the window. The curtains were drawn back, but there was no sign of anyone in there. In other words he had to prepare himself for a wait. Waiting took a long time, remarkably long it seemed, although he tried, and partly succeeded, to do some routine work, such as washing up, putting a load of washing in the machine, reading a little in a book, Thomas Mann's *Joseph and His Brothers*, which he held in high regard, but this idle waiting and unbearable tension, and almost panic-stricken fear that it would turn out that the suspicion he'd had, when he woke up in a daze in Trondheim earlier that day, had been justified, was followed by a tremendous feeling of relief when he caught a glimpse of a shadow that passed through early in the afternoon, in a room where the light still hadn't been turned on. Then the light was turned on. He felt relieved, although he couldn't be certain who was in there, but he thought it might be the youngish man who had been standing there on Boxing Day in the evening, though he couldn't be absolutely certain before the man appeared at the window. He did so not long afterwards, and it turned out that it was him. He was still there, then, and Professor Andersen could breathe a sigh of relief. But just then he was gripped by anxiety. Professor Andersen's reflexive consciousness surfaced suddenly and anxiety flowed through his body. For what was really about to happen to him? For the relief he felt now was actually frightening. Really it ought to have been quite the opposite. He was feeling relieved because he, the murderer, was still there. Imagine if Professor Andersen's suspicion in Trondheim this morning had been right! That he had vanished, and wouldn't turn up again, that he had just borrowed the apartment for Christmas and now had left it again, and quite simply disappeared out of Professor Andersen's life, what a relief that ought to have been! When that wasn't the case, but on the contrary quite the opposite, it made Professor Andersen extremely worried. He was concerned about himself, and more intensely than he could remember ever having been before. He was so concerned about himself that he noticed he was trembling and sweating from pure anxiety. 'I'm damned,' he thought. 'Now it has happened. I'm not able to go through with this.' But he couldn't put a stop to it. With alert self-scrutiny he observed himself as if through a transparent membrane. He couldn't reach himself through this film. He was, indeed, a damned soul. Behind this transparent membrane. He came home from Trondheim four days after Christmas Day, and up until after New Year's Day his powers of observation and concentration were directed at the window on the other side of the street, and at the figure inside, whom he was afraid would disappear from sight, since it might still be the case that he had just borrowed the apartment for Christmas and would disappear unnoticed, for instance with a small suitcase, for instance on 2 January, more than likely in the early morning. In this way he was tied to this murderer, of whom he had failed to notify the authorities.

Professor Andersen spent the last days of the year in his

apartment, alone and indoors, only interrupted by short trips out for newspapers, the mail, food and drink. He kept watch on the window over on the other side. He recognised him now. He even observed him outside as he went out of the main door of the building and along the pavement, before he disappeared round the corner of Drammensveien. Not with a suitcase or other travel bags, fortunately. This was repeated several times. He could be gone for hours, but he always came back. Professor Andersen didn't put on the light in his own living room, and was extremely careful not to move about in there in the few hours of daylight. But it was from the window here that he observed him, after the lights had been lit in the building on the other side of the street. He spent most of his time in his study, where he put on the light, but very often he stood behind the curtain in the dark living room and looked across at the window in the apart-ment in the building on the other side of the street, very carefully at that time of day when there was still daylight, motionless, on guard, so as not to arouse suspicion, something he didn't need to bother about after dark. It was in this fashion he moved around in his own spacious apartment, from the dark living room, through the equally dark dining room, to the bright study, where he then sat down for a while and pretended to read, before he got up and went back through the rooms in the apartment, brooding, self-scruti-nising, fully aware of what he was up to, but nonetheless shaken by the incomprehensibility of it.

'It isn't my not reporting it that worries me, or is it that after all?' he asked himself. 'Even if I can explain it. But why couldn't I seek Bernt's advice?' he thought. 'Why was I unable to let him, or someone else, in on this? That is the reason for it, that's what's behind it. The whole wretched mess, which is so extraordinary. It's more sinister than I like to think about. Who am I? Who is sitting and standing and walking here, and not knowing where to turn, making certain that a man whom I don't want to be associated with at all, with any of his misdeeds, doesn't disappear from sight? If he disappears, I'm free again. But I don't seem to want to be free again – that means something surely, but what?' reasoned Professor Andersen.

'I can't pretend I'm not doing this absolutely voluntarily,' he thought. 'Even if I feel forced to do it. I have tied myself to this misdeed, which I don't even dare think about, which has taken place in that apartment, after the curtains were drawn. Where is the body? The blood, all the shit, from the woman. The fair-haired woman, whom I think was young. What has that poor devil done in there? To be able to bear what he has done. Alone with the body. The blood (which he must have washed away, along with all the shit). Where is the body? It must be gone now, since the curtains are drawn back and the young man is going out in the evening and doing errands, whatever they amount to.'

'Life really lasts too long nowadays,' he thought. 'In our day and age. There is probably a lot to be said for meting out a man's life, all things taken into consideration, so it lasts about fifty-five years; then one has lived through the phases of one's life, without wear and tear. Childhood, youth, maturity, manhood, and then a short final phase. That should be enough, everything after that is an ordeal. If one is fifty-five years old the maturing process has gone so far that one ought to realise things are moving towards a rapid close. Then one would take that into account. That is the natural life cycle, which progress has wiped out, as if it were a germ, and thus made us ridiculously vain, childlike, both in mind and body,' thought Professor Andersen. 'We live far too long, both as children, as youths, in the years we mature, and as mature men. And even then our ordeals haven't started. The slow closing drama, fairly static, a horrible, slow end; the vainer you have been, the longer it lasts, this endless finale, the real face of modernity in the twentieth century. My life, in other words,' Professor Andersen added.

'Did I grasp the opportunity?' he asked himself, suddenly, 'Was that what I did? When I decided not to report it. It was terrible really, not to report it, that was what I didn't understand. I was blinded by recklessness, that's what I was. And am,' he added. 'Society exerts a tremendous influence over one. That was what I didn't understand, despite always having preached it – to my students, for instance. Why have I set myself up against society in this way? What is it I want to *see*? In myself? Or in him. He whom I saw murder?

'I can't defend it,' he thought. 'That's the heart of the matter. I'm not proud of it, not at all, but I couldn't have acted otherwise. The thought of informing on him revolts me, even if he is a murderer, that is a fact which I just have to take into account. I understand this, and stand by it. But why couldn't I tell Bernt about it, or someone else? What was it I feared in that connection? That I don't understand. Did I fear Bernt's arguments against it and his condemnation? I don't think so, for I know the arguments myself and agree with them. No civilisation can accept and defend the notion that someone who witnesses a murder could fail to bring it to the attention of society. It is surely the primordial crime. Even a father is duty-bound to report his son, and he does so, and if he doesn't, he suffers greater torment than I do now. I know all of this and am unable to disagree with it, but at the same time: I am also unable to report him. Not then and not now, either. Am I suffering from a boundless feeling of sympathy? In other words, compassion beyond all bounds? Am I suffering along with the murderer, and do I wish to continue to do so? But what about the murder victim? She is dead! Subjected to the primordial crime, but she is dead. The murderer is alive and must continue to be so. Along with me. Beyond all control, in secret. The murderer and his silent witness. The murderer who doesn't know about his silent witness, but is watched by him and observed. When shall we meet? What on earth is this? Why don't I want him to disappear from my life? Why do I fear that he'll disappear from my life?'

Agitated, Professor Andersen wandered around his

apartment and brooded over thoughts which didn't give him a moment's peace. No matter how much he brooded, he found no answers to his questions. He felt harassed and irritable over trivial irregularities in his routine, such as not being able to find the cheese slice, which he thought he had placed there, in the kitchen drawer, but which he found on top of the fridge, something which unleashed great irritation, directed at himself, because he lived alone and didn't have anyone else to blame when he couldn't find his cheese slice. It was New Year's Eve. The light was on in the window of the apartment opposite. Professor Andersen had purchased food and drink for a New Year's Eve alone in his own apartment. Fillet steak. Horse. A good red wine. Italian, a Barolo. At any rate, he would treat himself to a good meal, while he kept an eye on the man in the apartment in the building over on the other side of the street. He had also decided to read the latest Shakespeare translation by the poet Edvard Hoem, chiefly to see what misunderstandings were to be found in the translation or adaptation. He thought he learnt a great deal by studying the misunderstandings which were liable to arise when the English spoken by mysterious beings living in the Renaissance period was translated into Norwegian, a stubborn minority language in the twentieth century. 'Hmm, hmm,' he thought, with a sudden burst of good humour and anticipation. But then the light was turned off in the apartment. In that one over on the other side of the street. He saw it from his study, from where he had a sideways view. He went quickly into the dark living room and stationed himself behind the curtain. A little later he saw the man coming out of the main entrance, dressed up for a party in thin, black shoes and a thick overcoat with a white scarf slung nonchalantly around his neck. He saw him walk up to a waiting taxi and get in. The sight almost annoyed Professor Andersen. He felt a little offended. Here he was, forced to spend New Year's Eve all alone in a darkened living room, and then *he*, the other, goes out to amuse himself. 'But he won't amuse himself,' thought Professor Andersen. 'After all, he can't do that any longer. It's impossible for him, poor man. It's just a game he has to go through with because life has to go on as before, as though nothing has happened.'

Actually, he was glad the other had gone out. Henrik Nordstrøm, as he probably was called. It meant he was in for a quiet New Year's Eve. At any rate, until well after midnight, he could with certainty bargain on that. Indeed, why make plans for some imaginary hour after midnight? He definitely didn't need to sit up waiting for him to come home. He wouldn't vanish for good tonight; possibly tomorrow, or the day after tomorrow, but not tonight, he wasn't dressed for that. So New Year's Eve passed quietly. He laid the table in the dining room, and savoured his meal at about half past eight. Afterwards he sat down in his study with coffee and cognac and Edvard Hoem's translation of Shakespeare. He got out his English version of Shakespeare, along with a previous translation of the same play into Riksmål, in addition to the most recent translation into New Norwegian prior to Hoem's, and then compared Hoem's translation, or adaptation, to the others. To his great relief he was soon engrossed in this. He noticed a few doubtful things that Hoem had done, and pondered for a long time as to what he meant by them; in fact, his solutions impressed him a little, but he did wonder how the poet himself would explain them, and to what extent his explanation would stand up. Indeed, it would be interesting to meet Hoem one day and discuss Shakespeare translations with him, thought Professor Andersen, in as satisfied a mood as one might reasonably demand of him. When it was approaching twelve, he got up from his comfortable armchair and decided to go out, in order to hear the ships' sirens from the docks and watch the fireworks display.

Soon afterwards, he was on Drammensveien. It was a wintry night. The snow was frozen and hung on solitary city trees under the street lamps. The pavement was slippery, dirty white, and the night was, of course, dark. It was cold, but he had dressed warmly, apart from his head, which was bare. He didn't own a hat and he would rather not wear a cap, therefore he could feel the tips of his ears beginning to get cold. He walked briskly towards Tinkern Park, and followed the paths around it and over to the footbridge which stretched across the motorway between the sea and Skillebekk. Up there was a thick crowd of people, who were all out on the same errand as he was. He positioned himself in their midst, and soon the town-hall bells could be heard as they sounded twelve, followed by the sirens from all the boats in Oslo docks, and all the car horns from the taxis in Oslo city centre. The fireworks exploded in the sky in a powerful and entrancing spectacle. He heard people wishing each other Happy New Year, and champagne corks popping. From this footbridge over the motorway which passed right through Norway's capital city, one had a very good view of the fireworks which were sent up from most parts of town, from both Skillebekk and Frogner, as well as from Aker Brygge and the docklands. They sparked and whined in the dark winter sky and the rockets whizzed off into boundless space, only reaching the edge of it right enough, but seeing them whine upwards, small red and yellow shots of lightning, gave one a good impression of the boundlessness of space, even here where it began, before they exploded, and unfolded themselves in glittering harmonious formations, a real firework display, with lots of bangs and beautiful colours against the bleak and cold night sky. It was a joy to behold, not least because all the others thought it was so joyful, thought Professor Andersen with a little smile. He stood there for a while among all the festive people, before he retraced his steps. By then the time was half past twelve, and up in his apartment he had a good glass of cognac, both in quantity and quality, he thought, before sitting down in his comfy armchair for a little quiet reflection. He had another good glass of cognac, both in quality as well as quantity, he thought, and then another. It had turned half past one, and Professor Andersen had no wish to go to bed. So he decided to go for a night-time walk.

Professor Andersen went out for the second time that evening. He wandered in the streets round Skillebekk, where there was no longer anyone firing up rockets. It was cold and he noticed that he had too little on his feet. He really ought to have worn his boots and not ordinary shoes, even if they were thick-soled. Inside the apartments a surprisingly large number of lights were still on. 'This is one of the biggest party nights of the year,' thought Professor Andersen, 'now that champagne plays a part, people neither want to go home nor go to bed. Cheerful,' he thought. He arrived at Drammensveien, and began to follow it out towards Skarpsno. It was gone two now, and taxis continually drove past him, and the whole of Drammensveien became quite crowded with people who were walking home because they hadn't managed to hail a taxi. He walked along Drammensveien and passed a number of embassies. The Russian, the French, the stately English residency, the Egyptian, the Iranian, Israel's, Venezuela's, Brazil's. Had they also sent up rockets tonight? Professor Andersen wondered about that, and hoped so, for that would cast a reconciliatory light over everything, wouldn't it? 'Which I appreciate more and more as the years pass,' he thought. He turned immediately after reaching the park out at Skarpsno, and walked back again. He passed more people, who hurried home while they glanced sideways and backwards, on the look-out for an empty taxi. But the taxis which passed, and there were many, were all engaged. Outside his own building he remained standing for a while, relishing the fact that it was half past two in the morning and, although it was cold, he enjoyed being out so late. Then a taxi came to a halt by the pavement right in front of him, and *he* got out. The other. The murderer, who had now returned home. He walked straight past him, and Professor Andersen was able to see him up close for the first time. It lasted only a few seconds, before he bustled off across the street and unlocked the door in the gleam from the lamp outside the main entrance to the building where he lived. He fumbled a little with the keys, Professor Andersen noticed, but he wasn't unsteady on his feet. 'He's neither drunk nor sober,' Professor Andersen thought. And he didn't seem unlikeable, but neither was he the opposite, in other words, instantly likeable. 'This whole thing is strange,' he thought, but no more than that. Somehow it was a bit empty. But he noticed all the same that his knees were shaking as he walked up the steps to his own apartment.

Happy New Year, Professor Andersen! It's delightful to wake up to the New Year Concert from Vienna and the ski-jumping competition at Garmisch-Partenkirchen on 1 January in a new year. All of it on TV. Soon it will be work days at the university and slowly the days will get lighter. His name was Henrik Nordstrøm. He didn't leave his apartment with, for instance, two heavy suitcases, early in the morning, not on 1 January nor 2 January nor 3 January, there were lights in the windows over there, he lived there, permanently. It was his home. Henrik Nordstrøm. On 3 January Professor Andersen was back in his office at the university at Blindern, after the long Christmas break (at least as far as the university staff were concerned). Greeted colleagues, and received visits from the first master's degree students to arrive. He prepared his first lecture, which he was to give as early as 9 January. He noticed that the newspapers hadn't reported any woman missing whom he might have connected to the murder he had witnessed. He did observe Henrik Nordstrøm now and again when he left his apartment and stood at the tram stop and waited for a tram going towards the city centre. Professor Andersen had got into the habit of glancing across at the apartment on the other side of the street, but he had stopped standing concealed behind the curtain, and he had long ago gone back to normal lighting in his living room. But he had noticed that it was only in the morning that Henrik Nordstrøm stood at the tram stop and waited for a tram. Otherwise he got into a car, in the mid-range category, as they say, and drove off, or he took a taxi. The car he left standing parked outside the building where he lived, although rather a long way down the street, as a rule, on account of trouble finding a parking space, he presumed. As the weeks passed Professor Andersen grew more and more surprised. For there was still no woman reported missing who could be connected to the murder. The woman who had been killed was not missed. Evidently no one noticed the absence of the young, fair-haired woman. Why not? Was it possible that one could just disappear without further ado, and no one would notice? Professor Andersen thought that sounded strange, and concluded that the woman probably had been married to Henrik Nordstrøm or in some other way related to him, so he had been able to keep her disappeareance concealed. In that case, it would just be a question of time before the net tightened around him, as they say. And he must know that himself: the arsenal of excuses and explanations as to why she wasn't around any more, for instance, to family and friends, colleagues at work, if she had had any, would one day come to an end, or be worn so thin that they would unravel and suspicion would be aroused, for instance in the minds of the young woman's parents or of her brothers or sisters. It was just a question of time before he was caught. It occurred to Professor Andersen that *that* had been an assumption that he, Professor Andersen, had made the whole time. It was something he had reckoned with, as a certainty, and which had been lying there under all the emotions this case had aroused in him, and all the questions he had asked himself, regarding himself and his motives, in connection with it. He was dealing with a person in distress, someone fleeing from his misdeed, but one who knows that he will soon be caught. However, at the end of January and beginning of February there was still no one in the murderer's closest circle whose suspicions were strong enough to have had any kind of consequences for Henrik Nordstrøm.

Right from the start Professor Andersen had assumed that it wasn't Henrik Nordstrøm's wife he had seen at the window on the night before Christmas Day, but a casual female acquaintance, a girfriend of his, or suchlike. That was his assumption, on impulse, something he had never questioned before now, when it turned out that no woman was reported missing. He had expected that the description of this woman would be issued after a few weeks, fourteen days after Christmas Eve at the latest, in other words during the first or second week of January, and that he would then follow the newspaper reports about the search for this woman, how it slowly closed in on this apartment at Skillebekk, where Henrik Nordstrøm was sitting and tensely following the same hunt as he himself, Professor Andersen, in his spacious apartment on the other side of the street. But where was the body? Actually, Professor Andersen had imagined that one day, from his observation post, he would see two policemen entering the main door of the building on the other side of the street and ringing the doorbell at Henrik Nordstrøm's place. If the light was on in the window, he might be able to see all three moving about in there, the two uniformed men and the unfortunate Henrik Nordstrøm. But where was the body? Sooner or later suspicion would lead them to Henrik Nordstrøm but what could they do without the body? Probably very little. He, Professor Andersen, was the only person who had *seen* what had happened, and his lips were sealed. Why? 'And why did I leave the Britannia Hotel in Trondheim, head over heels, when I feared that he might simply disappear from here, for good?' Professor Andersen asked himself, yet another time, over and over again.

But as time passed what was most probable was that it hadn't been a casual female acquaintance, a girlfriend, who had been standing at the window, but his wife, whom he had murdered. That made the whole thing much more difficult for Henrik Nordstrøm, who, once suspicion had been aroused over the disappearance, would only have one opportunity to avoid being caught: if he himself reported her missing. If others reported her missing, Henrik Nordstrøm would, in reality, be finished. Even without the body. For as soon as she was reported missing, then it would turn out that she was, in fact, missing, and why hadn't Henrik Nordstrøm reported it? Viewed in that light it was now just a question of time before he was finished, and Professor Andersen's failure to report what he had seen wouldn't be of any consequence. He was finished, whether Professor Andersen opened his mouth or not didn't matter.

Between the months of January and February this had become quite clear to him, and it eased a little of the strain he had been living under recently. He now managed to concentrate fully on his duties as a professor of literature at the University of Oslo. True enough, Professor Andersen practised this calling in a context which didn't make him feel light-hearted. Indeed, the context in which he now found himself had darkened his existence, his mind even, for several years, and to an ever greater extent. When all was said and done, Professor Andersen had a strong suspicion that he had spent his life on something that was doomed to perish. He was a professor of literature and he could no longer say that there was as great a value attached to literature as he had thought at the time when he chose it for his course in life. At any rate, not the literature he had applied himself to in performance of his duties, but also for pleasure. He did research on Ibsen. He had completed an enthusiastically received doctorate on *The Pretenders* as a fairly young man, but in recent years had been preoccupied solely with the plays Ibsen wrote in the 1880s and 1890s, that is to say, with the great Henrik Ibsen. There could scarcely be any doubt that if Ibsen had died in the year 1880, at fifty-two years of age, he would have been forgotten as a playwright today. *Peer Gynt* and *Brand* would scarcely have been performed on any stage in the twentieth century, except perhaps in Norway. *A Doll's House* would also have been considered out-dated, if it weren't for support from plays like *Ghosts, The Wild Duck, Rosmersholm, Hedda Gabler, The Master Builder, John Gabriel Borkman* and *When We Dead Awaken.* His own doctorate on *The Pretenders* would have been regarded as a curiosity, and he would probably have been warned not to start on it, mainly due to the fact that a study of Norwegian drama around 1860 which took Bjørnson's historical dramas as a starting point would be much more rewarding, from both a historical and a literary perspective. So for that reason, throughout the past ten years Professor Andersen had been preoccupied solely with studying the great Ibsen, the Ibsen who made possible his doctorate on the (relatively speaking) forgotten work, *The*

Pretenders, and in consequence made his position as professor of literature possible, he thought, with a smile tainted by malevolence.

He had made use of all his imaginative and intellectual skills to depict Henrik Ibsen's dramas from the 1880s and 1890s, so that their greatness would stand forth in a shining light. As a professor he saw this as his task. What the students, whom he tried to enlighten in this manner, didn't know, was that he himself felt a gnawing sense of doubt as to whether this greatness actually existed, when all was said and done. He found himself having to take an extreme perspective in his interpretations, because if one couldn't view Ibsen's greatness in an extreme perspective, then one had to ask oneself whether there was any point in applying oneself to these dramatic works from the previous century, except in a strictly historical sense, which, of course, a nation ought to find a worthy cause, every so often. Take Bjørnson for instance, said Professor Andersen to himself. Even if there were people among us who only wish to be convinced of Henrik Ibsen's eternal greatness, and with that in mind go to the theatre to see a modernised Henrik Ibsen standing before them. One accepted everything, absolutely everything: inflated sex dolls, giant penises in plastic, Oswald as a neo-Nazi, long-haired punks, a peace negotiator with AIDS, a UN soldier stationed in Bosnia at home on leave, absolutely everything that one could imagine in the form of theatrical costumes to dress up poor fictive Oswald, all of it was swallowed if only one could perceive the eternal spirit of Ibsen breathing through this young man of our own day and age. As a professor, however, Andersen saw it as his task to concentrate on Ibsen's text, and search for greatness there. His students also yearned to feel the eternal spirit of Ibsen breathing on them. There were indeed master's degree students who spent up to two years of the precious spring of their youth immersing themselves in Ibsen's text. Why did they do that, really? On occasion Professor Andersen asked himself this, often sarcastically, too, if the truth be told. For why should a nice, amiable girl from Bærum be so fascinated by Rebekka West that she simply had to write a longish thesis about her in her own twenty-third year? Now and again it was beyond Professor Andersen's comprehension, not least her daring to admit it. Professor Andersen could safely say that he wouldn't have dared to admit it, if he were her, but she went around with her alleged enthusiasm for this intolerably sultry and morbid woman, not just at the university, but also in her circle of friends, indeed even in her childhood home, in the well-kept suburb of Bærum. Could it be that she was strangely fascinated by the thought of feeling Henrik Ibsen's eternal spirit flowing through this woman, whom she was going to devote a year and a half of her young life to describing? Yes, indeed, that had to be the case, and this made Professor Andersen's sarcasm creep away. For the fact remained that there were young students who yearned to apply themselves to Henrik Ibsen's one-hundred-year-old dramas and they flocked around Professor

Andersen's seat of learning. In his lectures they would hear the notion of Henrik Ibsen's greatness being confirmed and enlarged upon, in that way contributing to it being consolidated yet again for new generations, even though Professor Andersen himself did, in fact, doubt, ultimately, whether any such significance for which they yearned, and which he did his utmost to confirm, really existed; at least, it didn't for those people with whom he shared a common fate and the passage of time, for if one pared away all cultural yearning as well as vanity, necessary though it may be, both on behalf of himself, his day and age, and of humanity, and scrutinised the real enthusiasm in their heart of hearts for these masterpieces, for traces of a flame burning there, then he didn't expect to find any such flame. But he took good care to conceal these doubts from his students, as he might have made a fundamental error in those judgements that darkened his mind.

He himself had, after all, entered Ibsen's world, first as a student, later as a researcher and university teacher, without having experienced anything really momentous in relation to Ibsen's work. He had acknowledged his greatness as a fact, and thereafter studied him diligently. His master's thesis on *The Pretenders* (which he had later expanded into the enthusiastically received doctorate) had led him to study the play line by line, back and forth, weighing and measuring and comparing, so that he knew the work by heart and dreamed about it at night. All for the sake of a career, one might say. He had chosen Ibsen because it was sensible to do so if one intended to pursue a career in literary research in Norway, naturally enough. Later it had surprised him, he who so intensely despised careerists, and still did, that he himself had been so career-minded when he chose a topic for his master's thesis. He ought perhaps to have devoted himself to the literature he was passionately interested in, in his daily life, the poetry of our own century, but it hadn't occurred to him. He thought it was natural that a young man's master's thesis should be some form of training in dealing with the literary heritage, and that it was through training of this kind that one qualified oneself for doing research, hence for one's career. Therefore, he defended having embarked as a young man on Henrik Ibsen's dramatic work without having any particular attachment to it, and moreover that he had chosen one of Ibsen's early plays as the topic for this study lasting several years, first for his master's thesis, and later for his doctorate. For at that time the university was unchallenged as an institution, and demanded dispassionate adherence from its recruits. Today it was totally different. Everything Professor Andersen represented, and had represented, was challenged. Therefore, one had to defend oneself, and passionately at that. With composure and passion. Ideally, he regarded his task as that of contributing some footnotes to enable an understanding of Ibsen, a few footnotes, authored with passion. The more doubt he had concerning Ibsen's greatness – or concerning our ability to comprehend the genuine greatness of Ibsen in the 1880s with the same enthusiasm as one greets a mediocre rock star, or the anticipation with which large numbers of the population await the next episode of a TV soap – the more it fastened its grip on him, and became a part of the inner fibre which supported the 55-year-old professor, and set its stamp on his life and work, the more sceptical he became about his students' desire and ability to carry the literary heritage any further, through the humiliating intellectual life awaiting our kind of society in the next decades, and about whether there was any point at all in even trying, at any rate, under his supervision or guidance or direction.

But nevertheless one could see him displaying his ability at lectures and master's seminars, particularly the latter. Professor Andersen gave his all in order to demonstrate Ibsen's greatness in *Hedda Gabler* or *Ghosts*. In *Rosmersholm* and in *John Gabriel Borkman*. Not one word suggested that he himself doubted whether the play *Hedda Gabler* was great enough to survive for more than a hundred years, in its own right. Anything else is vanity on the part of humanity. He shook meanings from the text, pointed out the structure, the strange intellectual tensions and solvable paradoxes. He showed how highlighting various characters during the reading of the text, and looking at the play from their standpoint, as though they were the main character in the play, and then contrasting this with what happens if one lets another be the main character, and then letting these two interpretations stand side by side, allows one to see the void which then arises, the horrifying void; and he

referred to the crystal-clear emotional life one could observe
while Hedda Gabler moves from one room to another, from
one position to another, from a sofa to a fireplace with a
manuscript, from a living room to a lounge, where a pistol
is lying. All this with the students' full attention and vigilance. What they didn't know was that he followed them
with the same attention and vigilance, in order to reject or
in order to have his own suspicion confirmed, which lay
continually at the back of his mind throughout his concentrated work on *Hedda Gabler*, and which wasn't just a
suspicion that the play does not stand a chance of retaining
its force in our own day and age, other than as a poor
reflection of the original from 1890, but also to get rid of
the cynical question which continually accompanied his
inspired interpretations, and which ran like this, mockingly,
over and over again: 'Is this really all that good, when all
is said and done? That a general's daughter who marries
in a state of panic, and who gets bored, causes a damned
lot of trouble for others, and then finally shoots herself?
Is that something to apply oneself to, with all one's mental
faculties and emotional intensity, for centuries?' All this
buzzed in the back of his mind, like voices, while he carried
on lecturing, with his students' interests at heart. When
he had said something which he thought gave an exciting
insight into Ibsen's dramatic world, he waited expectantly
on his students' reactions. If they said something silly, then
it cut to him to the quick, likewise if all they could offer
were conventional statements picked up from some book

or other they had read, or some banal expression from the milieu they moved around in, or came from, or if any of them found it the right place to make known their own strictly personal emotional reactions, which they ought to have kept to themselves, because this was not a matter of emotions but of literary expression. But it did happen, and not all that infrequently either, that he could see someone's eyes light up a moment if he said something that sounded grand, and which he, Professor Andersen, couldn't deny actually referred to Ibsen's greatness, and then he noticed that a feeling of pleasure spread through his whole body, from the soles of his feet to the crown of his head, and not even his subsequent disappointment over the fact that the comments issuing from them, after this light in their eyes, were so insignificant, so facile, indeed so conventional, could quite oust it. And now and then a student whose eyes he saw gleam in such a way with enlightenment could make a comment that was a genuine expression of what had induced that glimmer, and could even present it with great feeling, and then Professor Andersen was moved as well. These were rare moments, but could be connected to the actions of Mrs Alving. Mrs Alving's actions which might be connected to the Greek tragedies, 2,500 years ago. As they might, might they not? Yes, Professor Andersen thought so, and he could present arguments in support of this, and then he could see the eyes of some students light up. They listened. Yes, they listened. Might one not trace a direct connection from a bourgeois Norwegian household, inhabited by Chamberlain Alving's descendants, in the 1880s, back to mythical Greece, 2,500 years ago? Yes, indeed. The stir was the same. In *Ghosts* as in the Greek tragedies. The stir which literature can cause. It was this stir that the citizens of Kristiania experienced sitting in the theatre the first time *Ghosts* was performed; it caused the same stir. Professor Andersen felt an inexpressible bliss on saying just this, to them, the students. 'But why have we lost this sense of stir, then?' he thought afterwards, when he was sitting in his office, and smoking, and trying to collect himself after this master's seminar. 'It is, in fact, much worse than I believed,' he thought then. 'We are only a hundred years removed from this stir, which down through history has been an elementary requirement for a rewarding life, and we can't grasp it any longer. So near, but all the same shut out. It's past. Are we shut out from one of humanity's most natural and most essential innate skills, which has been part of human nature, documented, at any rate, over the past 2,500 years? In that case a new kind of individual is about to emerge, and I am, whether I like it or not, one of its representatives, and my students, too, and they don't even know it,' thought Professor Andersen. 'My poor students,' he thought, 'who don't know this.' He thought about the gleam in their eyes when he led them from Ibsen down through history to mythical Greece and pointed out the connection. How they, subsequent to his pointing out this sense of 'stir', had sat down and compared Ibsen's play *Ghosts* from the 1880s with a 2,500-year-old tragedy by Sophocles, to find out how this could occur. Ibsen's dramatic form versus Sophocles' dramatic form, how drama had altered, over the centuries, and the perception of humanity and the portrayal of the people on the stage, too, their function there, everything had altered, but all the same this sense of stir existed, which it was possible to restore to the two plays, both Ibsen's and Sophocles', and that was what they attempted. Of course, Professor Andersen had been annoyed by the banal comparisons they drew, the conventional opinions, self-assertive sentimentalities typical of our time, but some of *their* eyes had lit up as well. From a longing for what would always be lost to them, and which they could now only preoccupy themselves with as a past phenomenon, which it is true could be studied with great intellectual enjoyment, by the most gifted, in good moments, as a shining example of how humanity had understood its condition, but without it applying to themselves, who could only view, and maybe also admire, this long period back in time when it had been in operation, before it suddenly had gone out of operation, right under their noses, so to speak? So that they were now forced – something he, 55-year-old Professor Andersen, was not – to go along with the new spirit of the times on its crazy and hubristic journey towards new experiences, new values, new constellations, new sounds, new cries, new criteria, new preferences, and all because they were young and on a wild journey towards a new era, with enthusiasm, whether they wanted to or not (that was what Professor Andersen escaped from, having to express enthusiasm for this, with rehearsed body movements, like a kind of dance, in the way he had noticed that young people couldn't avoid doing)? Professor Andersen felt compassion for his students, and wondered if it would soon be the right moment to stand up and voice his suspicion that the intellectual, reflective and bookish individual was now excluded for good. The reason why he did not do so was that in conjunction with this misgiving, out of the desire, or the duty, to stand up soon and voice it openly, something else lurked which was far more dangerous, and was absolutely negative. That no such stir existed as the one which Professor Andersen and his students had been studying today in Ibsen and Sophocles; that this was something which humanity had invented in order to endure its own inadequacy. True enough, for 2,500 years it had been necessary to maintain this illusion that human beings were creatures who allowed their inner selves to be stirred and moved by certain portrayals of the human condition, because although the ability was lacking both to create and comprehend such heights and depths in the understanding of human behaviour in order to understand their purpose here on earth, so there had been a yearning for this to be possible, but now it isn't there, 'and thus we can assume that no such stir has ever existed in connection with works of art created by man; these presentations have solely stirred us by virtue of their contemporaneity, the sensation that engenders, but have not had the ability to go beyond this. Now our wild course has brought us to the stage where we finally have the opportunity to rid ourselves of yet another illusion, one I would so much have preferred to keep, but I have succeeded in plumbing the depths of this suspicion, based on these very obvious assumptions,' thought Professor Andersen. He could picture the gleam in the eyes of his most gifted students, and thought wistfully of the times when this gleam had corresponded to a thought which so evidently had this sense of stir, if not as a personal experience, then nonetheless as its precondition.

Professor Andersen was in other words attached to his students, and to a much greater extent than they were aware. For he did not associate with them. After his lectures and seminars he shut himself away in his office, and spent his time there. But he was preoccupied with them, and he wasn't unaffected by associating professionally with so much youthfulness and, in better days, such a potential harvest. But he kept himself at a certain distance, he had always done that, and it had become more and more important to him over the years. But his eyes roved in their direction, and he thought about them often. For one thing, in recent years several students had cropped up who had something unmistakably familiar about them. There were features he recognised, and there were characteristic ways of making gestures, or ways of walking; they were the children of his own fellow students. And then he couldn't resist asking them whether it wasn't by any chance the case that such and such was the son of H. S. . . . , or the daughter of H. Kj . . . , and if the answer was yes, he felt great satisfaction. Being childless himself, he therefore got a certain pleasure from seeing new students crop up whom he could link directly to his own student days, thirty years ago, and in a way also to his own life, and not least because he was capable of discovering the connection. But occasionally he was wrong. When he posed his question as to whether it wasn't the case that such and such was the son of U . . . A, and the person in question didn't affirm it as he had expected, but replied U . . . A, who is that? or No, my father's name is N . . . B, then he became truly embarrassed, because, by doing this, he had tried to break into the intimate sphere of one of his students, which was how he then perceived it.

One afternoon at the end of February at around 3 p.m. he bumped into two of his students, two female students, on Karl Johans gate, right after he had left a board meeting at the National Theatre. He did that quite often, and he therefore stopped to exchange a few words with them. He asked them, because it was the done thing, how they were getting on with their master's theses, but they both burst out laughing, saying that he mustn't ask them today, because this was one of their rare days off. It turned out that both students worked in a wine bar when they weren't studying, each in separate bars, or rather wine bars, and that they weren't going to work until the next evening, and therefore were making the most of their liberty, strolling along Karl Johan in the pale, late-February afternoon sun, and they certainly weren't spending any time discussing their master's theses, instead they were discussing their customers in the wine bars, he understood them to say. 'So you're barmaids in your spare time, the two of you,' said Professor Andersen, being friendly. 'Yes,' they laughed, 'we're barmaids.' One of the female students suggested jokingly that Professor Andersen should come and visit the wine bar where she worked, he surely had time for a beer now and then, which made the other one equally eager for him to do so, the difference being that she wanted him to visit her wine bar, or pub, and not her friend's. Professor Andersen noted down the names and addresses of both the wine bars, and promised, without committing himself, of course, that he would do his best, because to tell the truth his life was arranged with such foresight that he had time for a beer or two. They parted and continued in different directions, the two female students on their way down Karl Johan, and he himself on his way up it, where he went through the Palace Park, before walking up towards Briskeby and after that down the whole of Niels Juels gate to Skillebekk, a rather roundabout route, which he enjoyed taking because the days were lighter now and there was, as already mentioned, some afternoon sun, which warmed him a little in the middle of winter. 'I really do believe I'll do it,' he thought to himself as he walked through the Palace Park. 'Yes, why not?' he added, as he walked up towards Briskeby. At the same time, he was a little startled that he was seriously considering what both he and the two girls had obviously regarded as a teasing suggestion, made in passing, while one exchanged some remarks because one had accidentally bumped into the other one afternoon on Karl Johan. 'No, give over,' he said to himself, while he walked down Niels Juels gate, 'this town has hundreds of wine bars you could go to if you want a beer, and many of them are much closer to your house than those names and addresses you noted down just now,' he added matter-of-factly, while shaking his head.

But he couldn't stop thinking about the conversation with the two female students. He couldn't stop himself going over and over it in his mind, when he was back home, and sitting in his study. There had been something merry about the two female students, which he couldn't just drop. They had tried to lure him in for a joke. They had begun to compete openly about possibly winning his favour, full of laughter, as a joke. And he had willingly allowed himself to be lured, as a joke, and had written down the names of both wine bars and in that way made it clear that he had nothing against being the object of their rivalry, and that this really was something he would consider. There was an undertone that he, one fine day, in the not too distant future, would crop up unexpectedly at one of the wine bars, and it might well be that he would actually do it, too, thought Professor Andersen, elated. It was in the spirit of the joke. One could turn up at only one of the wine bars. If he visited them both it would seem rather silly, as they would soon find out and the joke would be spoiled, he would have punctured it, and in that way made himself look foolish in their eyes, in not understanding a joke. If he were to follow the joke properly, he had to choose one of the wine bars, that is to say one of the female students, and then he would have pursued the ambiguity of the joke right to its final conclusion, which would be when he, Professor Andersen, cropped up at the counter in one of the wine bars and sat down there and let himself be served beer by the chosen student. Professor Andersen was so roused by this thought that he got up out of the armchair in his study and paced back and forth in his spacious apartment while he gave himself over to the fanciful idea, trying to decide which of the two female students he would surprise by suddenly cropping up in the wine bar while she was busy at work, in the bar, and then sitting down at the counter and ordering a beer, with a knowing expression on his face, yes, on his whole person. For he would then have shown that he had understood, and carried out, a joke in accordance with its ambivalent message. He had to admit that he had, to put it bluntly, become captivated by this accidental meeting with the two female students, and friends, on Karl Johan. By the two girls' joking insistence. By their closeness at the time. A spontaneous suggestion from two young girls. First one of them, out of the sheer joy of living, asked the professor to come and have a beer in the wine bar where she was a barmaid, and then the other joined in equally playfully, her throat full of bubbling laughter. Oh, he could imagine them now, all three, himself and the two female students who flocked around him, how they clamoured for his attention, threw back their heads and let out peals of laughter. If he had to choose, then he probably preferred the second one. Not the first one, even though it was she who had started the whole thing off, and who therefore could claim most of the honour for Professor Andersen being in such a frame of mind. Come to think of it, was it her, was that not the second one? It was after the second one joined in that the whole scene took on this strange innocence, bathed in an ambivalent light. If it had only been the first one, and the other one had remained standing a little self-consciously in the background, then the scene might easily have seemed rather blunt, and might have made him self-conscious, too. No, it was when the other one joined in and turned it into joking rivalry to win favour that it appeared to be pure and innocent, and the peals of laughter could trill out loud in Karl Johan, where they were standing, a professor and his two female students. So it was her he had to visit. Added to this judgement was also the fact that she, the second one, in contrast to the first, had been one of those he had seen with a gleam in her eyes in the seminar room at Blindern, when he had conducted the master's seminar on Ibsen and managed to trace the stir caused by art from Ibsen as a final port of call, for us at least, all the way back to Greek tragedy in its mythical landscape, in what we call antiquity, although she, as a rule, kept quiet during the following discussions. On account of the gleam he had seen in her eyes, he had been attracted to her shyness, and therefore he had been all the more surprised when she suddenly bubbled over in a teasing, joyful mood and appeared to be her girlfriend's rival in requesting that he favour her with a visit to the wine bar where she worked and not her girlfriend. He thought about the peculiar life she lived, her thoughts engrossed with the dramatic structures in *Hedda Gabler* during the day, and then acting as a raffish waitress at a bar during the evening. Thinking about this double life had the effect of making him intensely elated at the idea of paying her a visit in her bar, and in that way, within the bounds of a joke, sitting down at the counter and nodding knowingly to her, and that she would respond to this knowing nod by pouring him a ceremonial beer. Thinking of this forced him to sit down in his armchair and lean back, overwhelmed by this imagined agreement, which could become reality the moment he made up his mind to pursue the joke to its beautiful consummation. Professor Andersen didn't know exactly whether he would actually realise this fancy, but having the possibility open to him made him light-hearted this afternoon at the end of February, which had now become a dark evening. He therefore made up his mind to celebrate, so to speak, his good mood by going out for dinner. He fetched one of his Italian suits from the wardrobe and changed his clothes. He would relish having dinner at a restaurant round the corner from where he lived. A Japanese restaurant, which had an elegant sushi bar on the ground floor.

No sooner said than done. He set off round the corner

and went into the Japanese restaurant. In the bar stood a Japanese bartender or chef, making sushi dishes which he then served, one after the other, to the guests who were sitting around the bar and eating their sushi off a wooden platter. Professor Andersen saw that there were a couple of seats available there, and sat down on one of them. He ordered his sushi and a bottle of lager. A waitress soon arrived with the wooden platter, chopsticks and the lager. 'You ought to drink sake with it,' said the man who was sitting beside him. Professor Andersen turned towards him and said, 'Yes, I do believe you're right.' He beckoned to the waitress and asked her to change the lager to a small jar of sake. He then turned to his neighbour again, because he felt a strong urge to make it clear to him that it wasn't his first time in a Japanese restaurant, and that he was therefore well aware that this small jar of sake was an excellent drink to have with sushi dishes, but now and then it so happened that he preferred lager, just as he had tonight, but when his neighbour had suggested sake, he actually wanted that instead. He hesitated a little, right enough, before he embarked on this explanation, because at first he wondered if it wasn't sufficient that his neighbour had just heard him ordering 'a small jar of sake', which was the way it was served in this establishment, but as he didn't dare to rely entirely on this being sufficient rectification, he turned to his neighbour all the same. He embarked on his explanation, and then he suddenly recognised the man next to him, and to his horror he became aware of finding himself sitting beside the man whom on Holy Night, as we call the evening before Christmas Day, he had seen murdering a young woman in an apartment on the other side of the street from his own apartment building.

He was sitting beside Henrik Nordstrøm. He was staring into the murderer's face. He didn't know what to do. But he had begun his explanation, and he couldn't *not* complete it. He chose, however, to smile while he finished the explanation as to why he had chosen lager instead of sake, which he, as a rule, preferred when he was there. But when his neighbour, whom he familiarly called 'you', mentioned sake, he had such a great fancy for sake all the same, and therefore he called on the waitress at once and asked to change his lager to sake. 'Yes, that was the right thing to do,' said Henrik Nordstrøm. 'It has to be sake, in my opinion.' 'Not always,' said Professor Andersen, 'sometimes I prefer lager.' 'Well, yes, sometimes we do prefer to have a lager with whatever we eat, no matter what is really best with it,' said Henrik Nordstrøm. 'When I think about it, I mainly drink lager with meals when I'm in the Far East.' 'So you are often in the Far East?' asked Professor Andersen. 'Not any longer,' answered Henrik Nordstrøm. 'Before, but not now. Later, but not now. Now I'm here,' he said with a shrug.

Henrik Nordstrøm had the same kind of wooden platter in front of him, too. On it lay a couple of pieces of sushi, which he ate very elegantly using chopsticks. Shortly afterwards the Japanese bartender or chef handed the first piece of sushi over to Professor Andersen, along with horseradish and ginger. Professor Andersen began to eat. He dreaded it somewhat, as for one thing he was sitting beside the murderer and in this upsetting situation had to try to force down a bite of food, but also because he was a little uncertain about how he would master using chopsticks, which, after much practice, he could use more or less correctly, but he had never used them in such an upsetting and nerve-racking situation before. He concentrated intensely on this, and was relieved when his table companion didn't make any comments which might indicate that he now had some reason to believe that Professor Andersen wasn't really so familiar with Japanese restaurants after all, as he had just claimed. So Henrik Nordstrøm was still at large. He knew that anyway, for he could often observe him from the window of his apartment. Professor Andersen didn't understand how he had been able to keep his crime concealed for so long. Didn't the murdered woman, Mrs Nordstrøm, have any relatives or friends or workmates who missed her, or in some other way had become suspicious that something was not as it should be? He supposed Henrik Nordstrøm had managed to put them off with excuses, and with a story, which for the meantime was more or less credible and sufficiently reassuring for a relative or a workmate not to go to the sensational lengths of instigating a search for a woman whose husband had assured them of her good reasons for not coming to visit. But it was a dangerous gamble, and he was doomed in advance to lose. It was just a question of time. And that he knew, while he played this dangerous game. But so far nothing had happened, as yet no one missed Mrs Nordstrøm, or whatever her name was, to the extent that suspicion had been aroused and turned into manifest and vigilant uneasiness and anxiety, which demanded another answer. Now he was sitting here, in a Japanese restaurant in his own neighbourhood, and eating sushi in a sushi bar, along with Professor Andersen. They got talking and Henrik Nordstrøm talked willingly. For every piece of sushi that landed on Professor Andersen's platter, he had a comment to make, because he had just eaten the same piece, hadn't he, so he asked if his neighbour agreed with him that this bit was very good, in the circumstances, or whether he, too, hadn't tasted better. And Professor Andersen passed comment. As a rule he agreed with Henrik Nordstrøm, but now and then he took care to have an independent opinion, and then he might say, 'I've never tasted better scallops than this, at least not at this Japanese restaurant.' When Professor Andersen disagreed in this way, Henrik Nordstrøm opened his eyes wide and said, peeved, 'Well, that's your opinion, I have mine.' This way of opening his eyes wide and looking peeved, before dismissing it, wiping it out, was the most distinctive trait Professor Andersen could detect in Henrik Nordstrøm. Apart from his connection to the Far East, which he willingly made known, and willingly talked about. Small remarks about different places in the Far East, towns which Professor Andersen had never heard of, such as Siem Reap,

Mỹ Tho and Phitsanulok, seasoned, literally speaking, his comments on the pieces of sushi which Professor Andersen was eating, and which Henrik Nordstrøm had just eaten, and which made him remember different tastes from those Japanese tastes, the taste of lemon grass, coconut milk and fish from the Mekong Delta's inner reaches. 'In Japan the sushi is quite different,' he said. 'Oh, indeed, have you been to Japan often?' asked Professor Andersen. 'No, never, but I know that, because the sushi you get in Kuala Lumpur doesn't in the least remind you of the sushi you get here, of course not, it stands to reason, doesn't it?' 'Yes, it does,' answered Professor Andersen, 'but the sushi you get in New York isn't very different from what you get here,' he added. 'Apart from the mackerel, that is, and the cod.' 'I haven't been in New York,' said Henrik Nordstrøm, 'and actually I prefer Vietnamese and Chinese food, but you don't get that here in Norway, do you? And rarely in the rest of Europe either,' he added. 'It's only the name they have in common. I call that cheating.' 'I've been to Japan,' said Professor Andersen, 'for an Ibsen seminar. I've been to Beijing, too. For an Ibsen seminar, I'm a professor of literature,' he added. 'Oh,' said Henrik Nordstrøm, 'one wouldn't have guessed it from the way you handle your chopsticks.' 'It's good enough for me,' said Professor Andersen, annoyed. 'I manage to use them for what they are supposed to be used for, without having to pretend that I'm a native Japanese, or Chinese, for that matter.' Henrik Nordstrøm began to talk about something else. About the attraction the Far East held for him. About how a person who gets attracted to the Far East is never the same again. He had done business in the Far East. Roamed around in the Far East, in a way. Been connected to Norwegian companies there, in the Far East. Which companies? He hedged a bit. 'Statoil for one,' he answered. 'So you're in oil?' asked Professor Andersen. 'No, not exactly that. Was involved with other things. Been a kind of supplier,' said Henrik Nordstrøm. 'Supplying what then?' 'Different things. Whatever Statoil needs. Arranged contact between Statoil and suppliers,' said Henrik Nordstrøm. 'Well, not on my own, but along with some Americans down there. And also some Germans that I'm in contact with.' 'Whereabouts?' 'Vietnam,' he said. He preferred to talk about the mud, he said. The yellow mud in the Mekong river. About boat trips on the Mekong river. Sunsets on the Mekong. 'You become different in the Far East,' he said. 'There isn't anything mystical about it, it just happens to you. I'll soon be going down there again.' 'Where to?' 'Cambodia,' he said, 'or Campuchea, that's where things are happening, if you have connections. I can turn my hand to almost anything,' he added. 'I'm an electrician really. Or electrical fitter.'

Henrik Nordstrøm had finished his meal. He had requested, and received, his bill, and also paid, but he didn't leave. He sat beside Professor Andersen, commenting on the sushi the latter was eating. And talked about the Far East and his relationship to it. Professor Andersen finished the last piece of sushi and ordered coffee. The coffee arrived, and he drank it, while Henrik Nordstrøm sat beside him, without making any move to leave. While Professor Andersen was drinking coffee, Henrik Nordstrøm sat without saying much. He sat gazing into space, evidently lost in his own thoughts, or stealing a look at the other guests, who were mostly Japanese, probably connected to the Japanese diplomatic legation. When Professor Andersen had finished his coffee, he beckoned to the waitress and requested his bill. He was given it and he paid, and then stood up in order to leave. Henrik Nordstrøm got up, too, and together the two men fetched their overcoats from the coat stand and left the restaurant. As soon as they were out in the dark winter evening, Henrik Nordstrøm stuck out his right hand to introduce himself. 'Henrik Nordstrøm,' he said. Professor Andersen gripped it with his own right hand, and greeted him in the same manner. 'Pål Andersen,' he said. 'That was a lovely meal,' he said next. Henrik Nordstrøm nodded. 'But I miss not having a good Chinese or Vietnamese restaurant in this city,' he said. Professor Andersen nodded and began to walk in the direction of the building where he lived. Henrik Nordstrøm walked in the same direction. They walked around the corner and entered the street where Professor Andersen (as well as Henrik Nordstrøm) lived. Outside the main entrance to his building Professor Andersen came to a halt. He took his keyring from his overcoat pocket and searched for the key to the main door. He felt intense excitement running through his whole body. Now, it was now he had to make up his mind.

Now, right now. Hadn't this young man almost latched on to him from the moment he had accidentally sat down beside him? He couldn't flee now. Therefore he invited him up for a drink. Henrik Nordstrøm opened his eyes wide, looked at him in a friendly, but slightly ironic way, before saying, 'Yes, thanks, I'd love to.' Professor Andersen unlocked the main door and they went up the stairs to his apartment. They came into the hall and Professor Andersen showed his guest into the study, at the same time as he locked the door to the dining room. He told Henrik Nordstrøm to take a seat on the sofa. He himself went out into the kitchen and found whisky, seltzer and ice cubes. 'Goodness, what a lot of books!' Henrik Nordstrøm exclaimed when he came back in. 'Have you read all of them?' 'Yes, most of them,' answered Professor Andersen. 'Do you remember everything you've read, too?' 'Yes, most of it,' replied Professor Andersen. 'Is all that in there in your head?' said Henrik Nordstrøm, surprised, and gestured with his hands towards the bookshelves, which covered all the walls of the room. Professor Andersen nodded. He poured whisky and seltzer, and added ice. But when he handed one of the glasses to Henrik Nordstrøm, the latter requested a glass with just seltzer instead. 'Oh, I was quite sure that you drank whisky,' said Professor Andersen, apologetically. 'I do and I don't drink it,' answered Henrik Nordstrøm. 'There's a time and a place for every-thing.' 'Quite so, because I was pretty certain that you drank sake a while ago, so that was why . . . ,' said Professor Andersen in an almost unhappy voice. 'Yes, but that was then,' said Henrik Nordstrøm. 'Now I'd rather just have a little seltzer.' 'Yes, of course,' said Professor Andersen, and fetched a new glass for Henrik Nordstrøm, which he filled with seltzer and ice. He was a little annoyed. Why hadn't Henrik Nordstrøm told him that he only wanted seltzer when he saw that Professor Andersen was making two drinks with whisky and seltzer, instead of waiting until he was served the drink which was intended for him? And why hadn't he got up and left when he had paid his bill at the sushi bar, instead of remaining seated right until Professor Andersen had finished his meal, and paid? He made up his mind to come straight to the point. He told Henrik Nordstrøm about himself. That he had lived alone in his apartment for ten years now. That prior to this, he had been married for fifteen years. He talked a little about his marriage, although he disliked doing so, both generally speaking and in particular to this young man. But he had to tell him that Beate lived in the same town as him, though with a completely different name from the one she had had when she was married to him. Now she was called Beate Beck, and he hadn't seen her even once for ten years, because they didn't have any children together, after all, therefore there was no necessity for them to meet, and they had been spared any accidental meetings. He asked if Henrik Nordstrøm was in a position to know about marriage at first hand. Yes, he said, he had exactly the same experience as 'you, Pål, old chap'. Divorced, with a wife he didn't see any more, even though in his case it was only two years since they had separated. But his wife also had a different name now from the one she had had when she was married to him, for then her surname was Nordstrøm. Now she was called something else and was living in Hammerfest. He mentioned her name in passing, and Professor Andersen took note of it. Professor Andersen finished his drink and started immediately on the one that originally had been intended for Henrik Nordstrøm, while Henrik Nordstrøm merely sipped at his seltzer. There was something about the young man's appearance that he couldn't fathom. He was about thirty years old, of that he was certain, but where around that mark was absolutely indeterminable. At first he had thought he was younger than thirty, he was certainly twenty-eight, he had thought, but at the very instant that thought occurred to him, he had looked at him and had thought that no, no, he isn't twenty-eight, he's more than that, he's over thirty. He's thirty-two, he had thought, but when he regarded him in that light, then that wasn't right either, he wasn't thirty-two, he was much younger. So he was probably exactly thirty, then, since twenty-eight was far too young, and thirty-two far too old, and he looked at him and thought that he was exactly thirty, but he didn't think that could be right either, when he first looked at him, because then he thought, 'He isn't thirty, he's either somewhat older or else he's somewhat younger, I'm unable to decide which, although it's evident that he's either the one or the other, but he can't be what I think he is at a particular moment, because it's never right when I look at him.' Henrik Nordstrøm began to talk volubly about the Far East again. No one here in our country knew what was happening in the Far East these days, not properly; even those who were the best informed surmised only a snippet of it all. It is now at a great turning point, where everything is changing and bursting forth. It's teeming there. Everything's being transformed. And East is West, and West is East, and never the twain shall meet. Billions of people. Billions of people becoming the West in the East, If every Chinese was to eat an egg at breakfast, the world would come to an end. It's as simple as that. The world such as we know it, that is. It'll happen soon. 'When it has happened, these books can't tell you anything any more,' he said pointing at the bookshelves which covered the walls in Professor Andersen's study. 'And you who have all of that in your head!' he exclaimed. 'Poor you!' he said, shaking his head. Professor Andersen felt obliged to say then that no matter how things went, he considered it to be an advantage and not a drawback that he had all these books in his head. 'It might just be that one day it may give me a quiet sense of pleasure which will only be granted to a few people,' he said, and that made Henrik Nordstrøm open his eyes wide and stare at him with his young, indeterminable face. 'Well, well, it's everyone's right to believe what they like,' he said, after he had thought it over. 'But I like talking to you,' he added, emptying his glass of seltzer and standing up. He thanked him for the 'drink', as he called it, but now, unfortunately, he had to go. He had another engagement. Professor Andersen got up, too, and followed him to the door. As

Henrik Nordstrøm was about to go out the door which Professor Andersen was holding open for him, he asked if Professor Andersen had anything on next Wednesday. Because if he hadn't, he'd like to invite him to the Bjerke Racecourse. Henrik Nordstrøm owned a racehorse, along with three other people. A three-year-old thoroughbred horse which was to run the first race in its life next Wednesday. Professor Andersen was perplexed. He didn't know how to answer. He said that he didn't know if he had time next Wednesday afternoon, he didn't think he had any engagements, but was, after all, in a position where matters might suddenly crop up that required his attention, and which he couldn't ignore. 'Yes, well, let's do this then,' said Henrik Nordstrøm. 'I turn up here at your place on Wednesday at 5 p.m. and, if it suits you, then you come along.' Professor Andersen said that was an agreement, and they parted.

The minute Henrik Nordstrøm had left, Professor Andersen opened the door to the dining room, went through it and into the living room, where he stationed himself behind the curtain. He saw Henrik Nordstrøm come out of the main door and hurry towards his own entrance, unlock it and disappear in there. 'Uh-huh, another engagement!' exclaimed Professor Andersen to himself. He remained standing there for a while in order to see if a person really did come and ring the doorbell at the entrance of the building where Henrik Nordstrøm had his apartment. That did not happen. However, Henrik

Nordstrøm himself came out this same entrance a little while later and walked over to his car, which was parked outside, and drove off. Professor Andersen checked the time. Quarter past nine. Too late to phone Hammerfest? No. He called directory enquiries and asked for the number belonging to the name which Henrik Nordstrøm had said was the present name of his former wife. He called the number and a woman answered the telephone. She confirmed that she was the person bearing the name which Professor Andersen enquired about. And so he put down the receiver. He had his confirmation, and he didn't like it.

For now we are back where we started, and Professor Andersen is in a great fix. He is standing in his Italian suit looking at the telephone receiver, which he has just put back down on top of the telephone again, after getting the confirmation he didn't wish to get. That woman, who from his window on the night before Christmas Day he had seen Henrik Nordstrøm strangle in his apartment, was not his wife, but a strange woman. A woman who has not been reported missing and who probably cannot be connected to Henrik Nordstrøm in any particular way once she is found, or eventually reported missing. If, that is, she ever is. Professor Andersen was standing out in the hall where the telephone stood and was sunk deep in his own thoughts. He veritably sank down under the weight of them. Now he had returned to the starting point, and that felt worse than being stuck there around New Year's Eve. Everything that happened to Professor Andersen, from this evening until the murderer rang his doorbell the following Wednesday, appeared to take place in a kind of fog. Professor Andersen felt ill, so ill that in the morning he called the university and requested to be relieved of his duties that week. Afterwards, he went to a doctor, not Bernt Halvorsen, but another one, whom he had consulted previously, and he was granted fourteen days' sick leave. Strain. He sent notice of this sick leave to the university straight away. He was really unwell, his head ached, he saw spots before his eyes and he felt queasy all the time, but didn't throw up. He put on his pyjamas and went straight to bed. But he couldn't manage to lie still, so he got up, put on his dressing gown and wandered around his apartment, from room to room. This day, and the next day, and the day after that. While he brooded. And waited until next Wednesday. He had no idea what to do. His belief, or delusion, that Henrik Nordstrøm had murdered his own wife meant that he had thought the net was closing in on him, and that it could only be a matter of time before he was exposed, and that had reassured him to such an extent that he had managed to live an approximately normal life during the two months which had passed since he had witnessed the murder from his window. That had turned him into a kind of observer. Perhaps one could say that out of primitive curiosity he had kept an eye on the apartment across the street, and on its inhabitant, of late. A glance now and then, to catch sight of the man whose destiny would soon catch up with him.

But now he was back at square one. The murderer and himself, he, who had witnessed the murder. And who hadn't reported what he had witnessed, and who therefore was the reason why Henrik Nordstrøm walked around freely, without destiny catching up with him. And next Wednesday the murderer would ring his doorbell, so they could go to the Bjerke Racecourse together to see the murderer's horse running in its first race ever. 'I should have reported him,' he mumbled. 'Had I known what this would lead to, I would have reported him. If for no other reason than to know what really happened. Who was the woman I saw in the window on the evening before Christmas Day. Who is now dead. Why did he kill her? And what has he done with the body? And why has no one reported her missing? Indeed, I might be tempted to get dressed again and go to Majorstua Police Station right away, just to solve the riddle.' The thought raised his spirits, until it struck him yet again that this was just a flight of fancy, which gave him only a moment's comfort, and that he wouldn't seriously consider doing it. Even though he could now say he regretted not having reported the murder on the evening before Christmas Eve immediately after it had happened, when he had indeed gone to the telephone and lifted the receiver in order to call, it turned out – in spite of the sadness he now felt when he imagined this situation, when he lifted the receiver and put it back down again shortly after, without ringing the number which could have liberated him from what would later cause him such trouble and which now troubled him more than ever – when the thought of reporting it now arose, he was just as powerless as before. It had been and still was impossible for him to report Henrik Nordstrøm, even now, after meeting him. 'And I rushed headlong from Trondheim because I was afraid I would lose him. Good God! At least I wouldn't do that again,' he exclaimed. 'Wouldn't you?' he added hastily, 'are you quite certain about that?' he heard himself thinking, in a sarcastic tone. 'You've said that you don't know why you did that, haven't you? And if you don't know why you did it, how can you be so sure that you wouldn't do it again? Oh, leave off, leave off!' He walked round his apartment in his pyjamas, with a dressing gown tied at the waist to keep him warm. Now and then he felt far too hot, and he loosened the belt and let his dressing gown hang open. 'But,' he thought, 'my not reporting him is based on a single supposition, let that be clear. And that is the fact that it was a chance murder, not planned, but committed in desperation, out of a sense of injury, anger. If it had been a murder committed for the pleasure of it I wouldn't have hesitated in reporting it. Likewise, if it had been planned in cold blood. Oh no,' he said in dismay, 'I wouldn't have reported a premeditated murder. That's true,' he said quietly, 'I don't want to pretend. But a murder for pleasure, that I would have reported. But how could I know what kind of murder it was!' he then exclaimed. 'I only saw her being strangled; that was all I saw. But I have assumed that it happened in a frenzy, in blind fury, and thus blindly. Therefore I couldn't report him. I couldn't stomach doing it. Stomach?' he interrupted himself. 'Stomach, you say! Well, brain then. Consciousness. I couldn't bear to be the one to intervene so that justice could be done, as I assumed he was so appalled by his actions that I didn't want to prolong his suffering: better to relieve it instead, if that were possible. He didn't really mean to murder her. It was the act of a man who had lost his head. I might well have done it. You don't say,' he put in scornfully. 'You, who have just admitted that you couldn't have reported him even if you had known that it was premeditated. Could it have been you, then, too? Oh no,' he answered, 'I couldn't have planned a murder in cold blood. But I feel sorry for the person who has done it. It's unbearable to imagine oneself in his stead if such a dreadful deed, an atrocity, had been fully premeditated, yes, calculated. Therefore I want him to go free, escape, yes, maybe even forget the whole thing; yes, I do indeed, at any rate I can't assist in his arrest. But why then make an exception with regard to a confirmed murderer, my dear Pål Andersen?' thought Professor Andersen, splitting hairs. 'Because an unrepentant killer is dangerous. He can do it again. Ah but,' Professor Andersen interrupted himself exultantly, 'then you mean that someone who has planned a murder and afterwards carried it out in cold blood, without the least little bit of compassion for the person he has murdered or, even worse, is going to murder, isn't dangerous? Well, I must say!' he added. 'Yes, indeed, you must say,' Professor Andersen mimicked, 'but it is a fact that a premeditated murder is an isolated action carried out to solve a problem that must be solved, looked at from the point of view of the person who performs it, and which otherwise wouldn't have been solvable, and it is extremely doubtful, yes, statistically impossible, I should imagine, that one and the same person finds himself, or herself, twice in what is for them such an irresolvable situation, which may, in fact, be solved in this way. But an unrepentant killer murders because he likes to kill, and as long as there is someone to kill, then it's possible he'll do it again. Therefore, he must be reported so that he can be rendered harmless. Oh, I can't bear to think about it any more; no matter what I think, there is always something wrong. I only hope that he can get away, away from me at any rate, or vice versa,' he thought. 'Oh, I must get rid of him,' he thought, all of a sudden. 'Now, now, I didn't mean it in that way,' he added, and almost had to laugh. But the thought made him feel like laughing, and he had to repeat it. 'I must get rid of him,' he thought, and almost had to laugh again. 'Indeed, not in that way though,' he added, and now he really had to laugh. He laughed so much he couldn't stop, and started coughing. He laughed and coughed and between the outbreaks of laughing and coughing he thought, 'I call that a morbid sense of humour,' and the hiccups of laughter broke out again, so that he walked around his apartment bent double, from room to room, in pyjamas, with a dressing gown over. He wasn't barefoot: he was in his socks, because he didn't want to catch influenza, on top of it all. Professor

Andersen never wore pyjamas, for that matter, except when he was ill, as he now was, though he lacked the peace of mind to lie quietly in bed. He had just one pair of pyjamas, the ones he had been given many years ago by his long-departed mother, and which he hadn't worn much, as Professor Andersen was rarely ill. He walked through the rooms in his apartment, at his wits' end. He looked at the books on the bookshelves lining the walls of his study. He was pale from the laughing fit, which he now regarded with great concern, as it was an expression of emotional agitation by a man standing on the brink of something or other. All those conflicts he had read about, all those men under duress, at crossroads, forced to make a choice, metres and metres of books on the shelves dealt with just that, but these could not help him at all now. 'Oh, but I have learnt nothing,' he sighed, 'because there is nothing to learn; I have all these books in my head, as I pointed out to the man who is behind all these troubles, but not literally speaking, after all. If that were actually true, I couldn't have opened a single cupboard in this apartment without old skeletons falling out, and that isn't how it is, after all. I can prove that, just by opening a cupboard,' he thought. 'But don't do it,' he added, 'not now, in the state you are in.'

Professor Andersen paced round his apartment, from early morning to late at night. At midday he usually lay down in bed and, as a rule, he then slept for a few hours, in a kind of doze. The same at night. He slept fitfully, his dreams reduced to muddled thoughts, milling around. Nevertheless, he felt alert as he wandered restlessly around the apartment, and he also passed the time by doing daily chores, such as making food, eating, washing up, vacuuming, tidying. Indeed, he even made the bed, although he knew that he was going to lie in it most of the day, and that he would lie down in it again in a few hours' time, for a rest of sorts after dinner. He felt his mind was crystal clear, but despite that he was at his wits' end. He couldn't understand his reluctance to report Henrik Nordstrøm for the murder he had seen him commit. Well, yes, he understood that he hadn't reported him when it had happened, but why he was unable to report him now, when he had experienced, bodily and mentally, the impossible consequences it held for him was more than he could fathom. His sin of omission couldn't be defended. Every civilisation is built on such actions being indefensible. That goes without saying. In all circumstances. When he didn't report it, he had become an outcast, along with the murderer. An outcast in his own eyes, along with the murderer. And he deserved this. And behind it all was God. As the ultimate reason why breaking this natural order was a taboo which no living person can explain, touch or wipe from their memory. Professor Andersen was not a religious man, he was fairly unfamiliar with thinking along those lines, but now he couldn't stop himself blurting out, when he thought and thought about what he had become entangled in, and couldn't get untangled from, even though he desperately wanted to, 'No one can have their own

God. Not even the godless.' He was startled when that thought struck him. But he was forced to realise that it was self-evident, and that he had no alternative but to take heed of it.

The thought had emerged completely spontaneously, as a vision, which had burst its way through his broodings, as he paced around his apartment, in pyjamas, with a dressing gown on, right in the middle of the day. It was an inner voice which called out, and he felt both taken by surprise and uncomfortable. It wasn't the first time he had been entangled in a train of thought that made him feel uncomfortable, and which he didn't like. Ever since the murderer had entered his life, he had had a tendency to get hung up on impossible abstractions, ones which quite simply made him feel sick. For instance, having made up his mind, urgently and repeatedly, that Henrik Nordstrøm had commited a 'primordial crime', he could find himself staring intently at his watch in order to see, or feel, if there might be a connection between 'primordial time' in the sense of early origin, and 'time' as measured by the apparatus which ticks your own time and which is strapped around your wrist. It was, in any case, a connection which Professor Andersen found repulsive and far from fascinating, particularly because he was the one who had been distracted by such a notion. And it was probably this resistance in his own mind to speculative thinking which had made him so immune to metaphysical and religious thinking, from his twenties onwards. He might indeed listen with interest when others expressed metaphysical ideas, but if they cropped up in his own head, in his own work as it were, he was repulsed. But this time he wasn't. He didn't discard the thought immediately, as he usually did, but found that he had to take it into account, as existing in his mind. For several months now he had been troubled by the thought of lifting up the telephone receiver, only to lay it down again, because he couldn't report Henrik Nordstrøm for the murder of the young woman, which he had seen him commit, and afterwards he constantly felt the blast of society's demands and noticed the strength of society's effect, even on its essentially disloyal servant, Professor Pål Andersen, dizzy at the thought of what he had done, or neglected to do, and at the meeting with the murderer, which he couldn't rid himself of, and which made him exclaim, addressing his inner self, crying out loud, 'No one can have their own God! Not even the godless!' and as he voiced this in his mind, it seemed to him to be so self-evident and correct that he was startled, while at the same time he felt uncomfortable, even dejected, about his own manner of speaking, which had appeared so spontaneously, and had been his own work.

By doing so, Professor Andersen had recognised God: not God's existence as such, but God as an abstract concept, and as a necessity which goes beyond social considerations, but all the same an abstraction of the kind that could in the final instance issue Professor Andersen with a kind of divine command in connection with the difficult situation into which he had manoeuvred himself on account of his sin of omission. At the deepest level of meaning, in the ultimate instance, God had appeared, and in Professor Andersen's mouth. He just had to affirm that. Accordingly, Professor Andersen was fully aware of what had happened to him. Despite his dejection arising from the manner of speaking he had spontaneously adopted, this recognition by no means needed to cause any radical change in his life, as he had lived it up to now. His self-evident thought did not require him to kneel down or pray or adopt a false mildness in his normal manner of behaviour, or any pious church appearance, or denial of life, or meekness, only a certain awe and respect for the divine dimension of exist-ence. It also required him to do his duty with regard to the 'divine command', which he had just recognised. He was also able to admit that this self-evident thought could be seen as liberating, since it involved a divine dimension in one's way of thinking that ought to have a broadening rather than a limiting effect on one's consciousness. He understood all of this immediately, but all the same he had felt dejected, because of the form of expression he had used so spontaneously, which was such an exact expression of the thought that had appeared so readily and aptly in his brooding, indeed haunted, mind. Instead of counting himself fortunate for gaining insight into the necessity of God in that way – without even seeking such insight! – he felt uncomfortable. Because he couldn't follow the 'divine command' demanded by this undeserved insight into the necessity of God. Because it would have led him to set off for Majorstua Police Station and report Henrik Nordstrøm for the murder he had seen him commit two months ago. And he still couldn't do that. Not because it would now have been downright embarrassing to enter Majorstua Police Station and say that on the night before Christmas Day last year (last year! sic!) he had seen a murder from his window, and that the murderer's name was Henrik Nordstrøm, and that the murdered person was a young woman with fair hair; mind you, that's what it was, extremely embarrassing, as it was unlikely there would be any trace of this murder: no body, and no woman reported missing who could fit the description. But it would have been possible to live with that. Henrik Nordstrøm would have got away, and he would have been left standing with his excuses; both of them would have been regarded as 'suspicious characters' by the police force, and that would be all. But at any rate he would have reported it, followed the 'divine command', and in that way confirmed that he had understood the words he uttered when on the extreme brink. Nonetheless, he couldn't report him. It was impossible for him to do it. It was out of the question. Divine command or not, it was impossible for him to do it. And thus his insight came to no avail, this strange, undeserved gift of grace was completely wasted on him, if one wished to interpret it in that way, and Professor Andersen was certainly not unfamiliar with that way of interpreting it, because he had received his own rather surprising words, directed inwardly at himself, with great awe, even if they had also made him dejected, but this dejection lay precisely in the fact that the words he had expressed so spontaneously had issued from the lips of a man who was utterly unable to appreciate them, when all was said and done, it turned out, because he wasn't able to do so.

When Professor Andersen realised that he wasn't able to report Henrik Nordstrøm, even on account of a divine command, he grew annoyed. 'But it is just ridiculous,' he thought, 'really, all I want is to report the guy. It would be a relief pure and simple and now there's nothing to stop it, either. What on earth is the reason that I'm unable to do it? It's just stubbornness and inflexibility,' he thought, irritated, 'an insufferable obstinacy that is in my mind, unfortunately, and sets its mark or holds it upright, as I'm certainly leading myself to believe. It is quite insufferable. If only I had one sensible reason, but I haven't. All the reasons I have or have had, I have removed at once, so that I'm left standing naked and almost trembling,' he mumbled. 'What am I trembling for?' he thought, dejected, shaking his head while he walked restlessly around the apartment, still in pyjamas and dressing gown, in the middle of the day. Now and then he suddenly came to a stop, and remained standing dead still, in the middle of the room, motionless, and he could remain standing like this for several minutes, while he was thinking, as far as his wits would allow him. 'Perhaps my poor arguments are an expression of my not *daring* to face the real reasons on which I base this decision,' he thought quietly. 'What on earth can they be? Why do I say that it isn't right to report him? I must mean it, after all, since I maintain it so strongly, without a proper argument.'

He went through it all once again in his mind. A murder has taken place. The murdered person is dead; the murderer is alive. It was not the murderer's responsibility, but the murderer's consternation that it hinged on, that was undoubtedly how it was, viewed from Professor Andersen's angle, therefore he had laid down the receiver again, after first lifting it up, after he had witnessed the crime and rushed to the telephone, which stood out in the hall on a little table there. When he now thought carefully through all this and urgently asked himself 'why?', he noticed that he had a tendency to refer to his actions, or lack of action, in turns of speech which were clearly erroneous, such as answering that he didn't want to 'inform on' the murderer, or that he didn't want to 'add stones to his burden', something which, on second thoughts and subjected to critical testing, couldn't stand being presented openly as sensible reflections. 'To report a murder one has seen isn't informing,' thought Professor Andersen, slightly taken aback at having to go to the lengths of putting himself right about such an obvious matter. But such notions as these were lodged, quite entrenched, in his consciousness. 'I don't want to stone him,' he might catch himself exclaiming in his own defence, 'it's too primitive.' He then had to admit that deep within him was the notion that there ought to be something primitive about the act of reporting that one has witnessed a primordial crime, because this notification would lead to the criminal's arrest, with criminal proceedings and punishment. It ought to mean 'throwing the first stone'. If one set these notions against the clear, self-evident idea Professor Andersen had thought of quite spontaneously, and which involved a recognition of a divine principle, with which he was now faced, and had to see his own sin of omission in light of, Professor Andersen had to admit that this indicated that he did have a notion that this insight into the necessity of God was strongly interwoven with the feeling that he was now standing face to face with the Desert God, and that it was the Desert God's command to stone the murderer, even throw the first stone, which he so strongly hesitated from following. A primitive feudal God orders Professor Andersen from the university at Blindern in Oslo, the capital city of the modern state of Norway towards the end of the twentieth century, to carry out a primitive action ordered by God. 'No wonder I hesitate,' he thought, 'but the fact is that it doesn't add up. I haven't met the Desert God, and the action I have been commanded to carry out isn't primitive, but necessary in order to uphold civilisation.'

All the same. Professor Andersen wasn't able to report him. No matter how easily all the arguments for not doing it were punctured and exposed, reporting him was out of the question. 'It makes me furious,' he thought. 'I get disgusted at the thought. I don't want to be the person who does it.' Even if he could show that by focusing on the murder victim, the young woman, and envisaging her last seconds, which he *saw* with his own eyes, when she knew that she was on the point of losing her life, being murdered, strangled by a man she knew, indeed was celebrating Christmas Eve with, the pain and the completely incomprehensible and, in her case, irreversible, nature of this, then there was nothing left which could justify any sympathy or pity for the person who had done it; 'It must have been terribly painful,' he exhorted himself, 'both bodily, and not least mentally. No human being should be allowed to inflict such fear in another person and go unpunished,' he cried out inwardly. 'Admit at least that it is rash of you not to report him,' he pleaded. But to no avail. For Professor Andersen she was dead, and no punishment could make her rise up again and reappear at the window of the apartment on the other side of the street, where she stared out, on the evening before Christmas Day. His concern was for the murderer, the person who was left there, with the body in front of him, the murderer chained to his own misdeed, which he had witnessed.

The murderer, with his misdeed, and Professor Andersen, who has seen it. Professor Andersen snaps his fingers and the murderer gets up, draws the curtains and removes the body, washes away all the traces, and on New Year's Eve, at seven o'clock in the evening, one can see him walking calmly out of the main door of the building he lives in and seating himself in a taxi and driving away, before he, as though nothing has happened, comes back, in another taxi, at two o'clock in the morning, on New Year's Day, and walks up to his own place again, not sober and not drunk. Professor Andersen has snapped his fingers, and a murderer goes free. Professor Andersen smiled to himself. He had given his answer. This was it. To snap one's fingers. Professor Andersen felt a sense of relief stealing over him, almost blissful, at the thought of what he had done. He had reconciled himself to his deed. The moment he thought of how he had snapped his fingers, he knew that he knew what he had done, and that he had reconciled himself to his deed. Now he would sleep, even if it was the middle of the day. He would dive into bed, lay his head on the pillow, shut his eyes and give himself over to sleep, and to all the dreams, good and bad, where anything can happen. 'I'm not afraid to sleep,' he thought, 'despite all the nightmares I've had over the years, right from the time when I was a little boy. I never think about them when tiredness overcomes me and I just want to sleep, even though I know that I risk waking up, immersed in fear. I know that, but I don't think about it, it's a little strange,' thought Professor Andersen, while his 55-year-old face lit up with a broad smile. He felt tired and liberated. But he no sooner felt tired, and liberated, than he noticed that he had become uneasy. 'That was very simple, then,' he thought. 'Snapping one's fingers, and then I am reconciled to my deed, and know that that was why I couldn't report him. But it is true, though,' he added, 'yes indeed, it's true. But it's terrible, though!' he then exclaimed.

'A snap of the fingers and then I've sundered myself from God,' he thought. 'Well, I must say, I didn't believe it was as simple as all that. But that's the way it is, then. And what can I do about it? Nothing. It's as though I'm standing outside myself, just observing. Dare I say with a shrug? No, I daren't say it, because it's not true. Oh, now I know why I couldn't confide in Bernt!' he exclaimed. 'I had thought it might be because I feared his disapproval, but that didn't add up, as I couldn't imagine Bernt disapproving, when all was said and done, not seriously. Of course, it's the opposite way around. I couldn't say anything to him because I was afraid of him approving of it. I couldn't stand him approving of it. Least of all for Bernt's sake. But also for my own sake, it would have made me so lonely. I had done what I had done and I couldn't undo it, but I couldn't stand the thought of Bernt approving of it, and thus abruptly: my own terrifying loneliness. I don't discount that, strictly speaking, Bernt would have dissociated himself from it, on account of public morality, and he would have requested me to consider the consequences, to see the whole thing from the murdered young woman's point of view, but there would have been something half-hearted about the way he spoke, I'm certain of that. I wouldn't have been able to avoid noticing the respect for my action on his face, indeed his partial, and secretive, admiration, because the fact that a person with cancer rots away and dies suffering violent pain, only just alleviated by morphine, that is something nothing can be done about. But to let the murderer get away, in any case, at least between ourselves, is a secret wish. But no one can have their own God, not even the godless,' cried Professor Andersen. 'At least, not without being damned. And doomed to stand and contemplate damnation, because no one is able to entertain a feeling of admiration, not even in secret, for their own ability to snap their fingers, when the opportunity arises, so that the murderer can get up and flee from his misdeed, and in that way make an eternal protest against the unbearable cruelty of existence, indeed, its meaninglessness. I must already have realised it at the time,' thought Professor Andersen, 'that Bernt Halvorsen's secret admiration would have appeared meaningless to me, because it brands my action as understandable, something I would have been unable to tackle in my desperation. Because I had witnessed the murder and been negligent with my eyes open, I had sunk into a state of desperation which had long ago transformed my action from an apparent revolt into a form of damnation. But I didn't have words for it then. And Bernt wouldn't have comprehended it either. Serious Bernt Halvorsen, with his high ethical standards, wouldn't have understood a word of what I wanted to express, even though he would have done his utmost to attempt it, and in purely logical terms he might even have made some comments about it, being such an obliging man, so that we might at least have been able to conduct some kind of conversation about it, since it was so evident that it meant a great deal to me, not least dressing up my thoughts in this religious-coloured language, which I wasn't actually capable of doing at that time. Yes, really,' thought Professor Andersen, 'I can well imagine what would have happened if we had informed all the dinner guests, telling them what had happened to me, as each of them arrived, on Boxing Day two months ago; Trine Napstad and Per Ekeberg, Judith Berg and Jan Brynhildsen, along with Nina, who would have been the first one to be told, and all of them would have reacted in the same way. Requested me to consider the consequences, and urgently appealed to me to go to the police and report what I had seen, but all the same, among all of them, a secret wish that I didn't have to listen to them, something they would have confirmed, making solemn vows of secrecy, in case I didn't follow their urgent appeals.' He had held his tongue, because he couldn't talk about damnation then. He himself had had no words for it then, and if he had had words for it at the time, then they wouldn't have understood them. They would have retained their secret admiration, even if he had said that he was damned, for being damned, the way he regarded it at the time, in all his wordless desperation, would have appeared so strange to them, so odd, that they wouldn't have been able to take it into account. 'And that's how I feel about it, too, now, at this moment,' thought Professor Andersen, 'that it's strange, odd, even though I know I'm damned.

'But can I be damned when I don't believe in God?' Professor Andersen asked himself. 'Because I don't, since it's impossible for me to follow the divine command. Oh, it's no use,' he sighed, 'because I do, indeed, feel damnation now, I'm not able to conjure it away. I don't even feel frightened of sticking my tongue out at God, and no one would be shaken to the depths of their being if I were to announce that. It's quite simply a strange idea to imagine that I have committed a sin of any kind. I can relate to the notion of damnation, but not to the fact that when I snapped my fingers and let a murderer off, I sinned against God. It's strange, odd. And I'm freezing cold. I've gone beyond a limit, and when I passed it, I met something I found necessary to address as God. It was freezing cold and strange. No, I don't want to stay here. I'll shake it off me, turn round and walk on, home again, if I may say so,' thought Professor Andersen.

At that very moment the doorbell rang. Professor Andersen almost jumped out of his skin. Who could it be? Then he realised. Next Wednesday. It was next Wednesday. He went to the front door and opened it. There was Henrik Nordstrøm. Professor Andersen greeted him in the doorway, attired in his dressing gown over his pyjamas. 'I've been ill,' said Professor Andersen to the man across the threshold. 'Have been, or are?' asked Henrik Nordstrøm. 'I don't know, really,' smiled Professor Andersen, as he leaned against the door, which he held ajar. 'If you are going to come along, then you have to hurry up and get changed,' said Henrik Nordstrøm. 'No, it's not possible, because if I am well again then I have a lot of work to catch up on.' 'Then you're not coming, I take it?' said Henrik Nordstrøm, and looked at his watch. 'No, I'm sorry, it's just not possible.' 'Very well,'

[152]

said Henrik Nordstrøm, 'that may be, but it would have done you good to come along. But maybe another time.' 'Yes, maybe another time,' answered Professor Andersen. He thought he would wish Henrik Nordstrøm 'good luck' with the horse, in order to round off the conversation in that way, but he couldn't bring himself to say it. Instead he thought that he would say 'take care' or 'goodbye', but he couldn't bring himself to say that either. Then Henrik Nordstrøm looked at his watch again, turned round and went downstairs. Professor Andersen heard his rapid foot-steps on the way down. Suddenly, he thought of something and hurried over to the banister, leaned over it and shouted to the man who was on the point of disappearing, 'When are you going to leave, by the way?' 'Leave?' he heard the other man's voice calling up to him. 'Yes, for the Far East?' 'Oh, that. Any time now. In a few weeks, perhaps in a few months.' 'What are you going to do with your apartment? Sell it?' 'Sell it? What for? I'll be coming back. At some point. Perhaps rent it out, or I may just leave it empty. My sister can always stay there, when she comes to Oslo.' 'Yes, that sounds sensible. Are your parents alive?' 'My parents? What makes you ask that?' 'Well, I don't know, it was just something that struck me. But I can't stand here in the corridor any longer,' he shouted to the man below, 'for I'm starting to shiver. It would be silly to catch the flu right now, when I'm beginning to get well.' 'Yes, take care, and read the results from the first race at Bjerke in the news-papers tomorrow. The horse is called Sugar Pile, and you can look for that name at the top of the page.' 'Yes, I'll do that,' said Professor Andersen, 'but now I must go in and have a warm bath.' With these words he went into his apartment, locked the door and continued to pace restlessly around the apartment. 'Perhaps I should do that?' he thought after a while. 'Do what?' he asked himself. And he came to a halt. 'Have a bath,' he replied, to himself. 'Yes, why not?' he added. 'A really hot bath, that would certainly do me good,' he thought.